THE HOPI WAY

THE HOPI WAY

Tales from a Vanishing Culture

Collected by Mando Sevillano

Line Drawings by Mike Castro

NORTHLAND PRESS · FLAGSTAFF, ARIZONA

FIRST EDITION

ISBN 0-87358-413-9
Library of Congress Catalog Card Number 86-61067
Composed and Printed in the United States of America

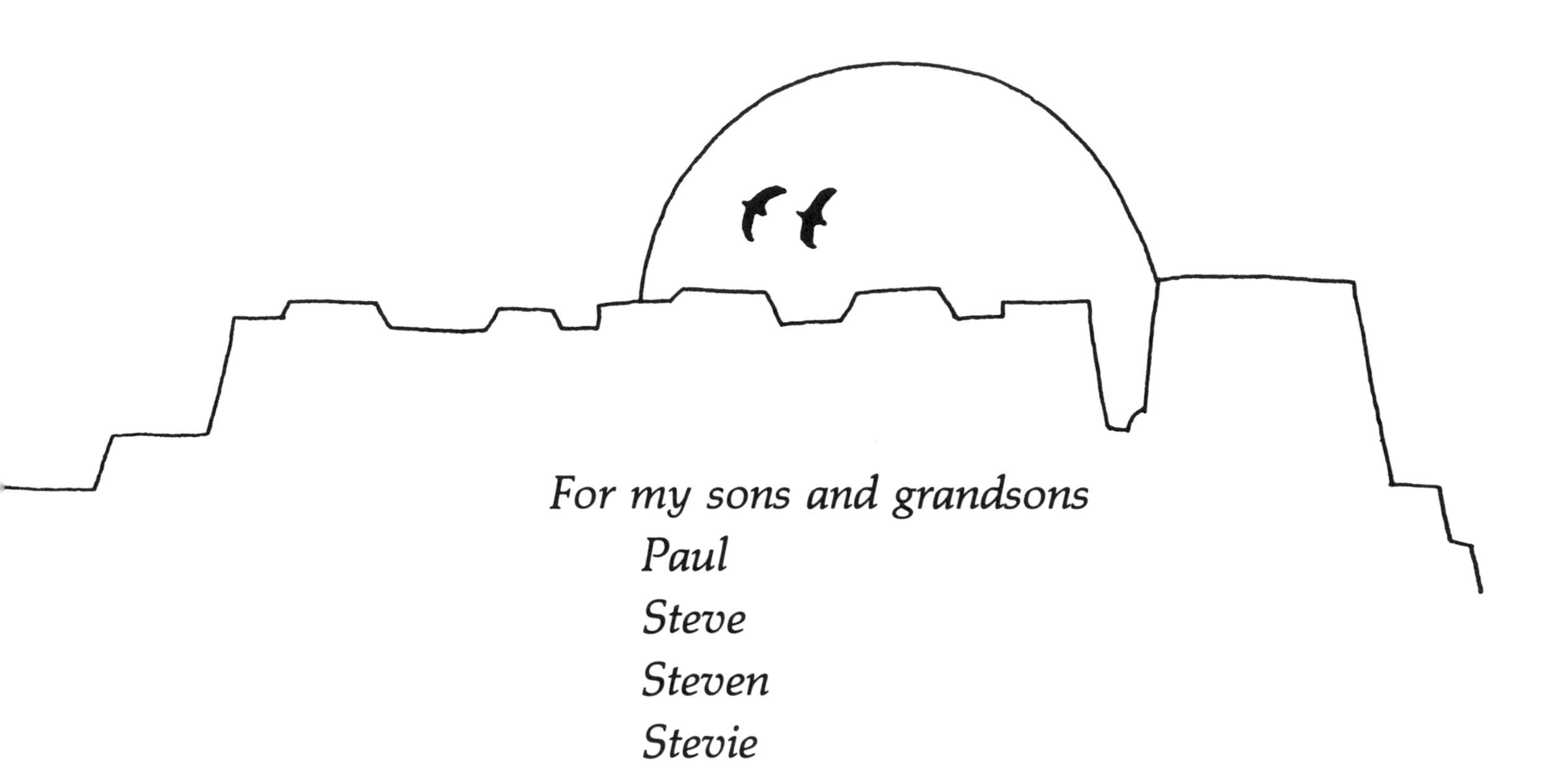

For my sons and grandsons

Paul

Steve

Steven

Stevie

Contents

Preface

This book contains seven Hopi teaching stories from First Mesa. Three of them, "Poowak Wuhti," "Hano Wuhti," and "Awatovi Story," are translated into English from the Hopi language. The other four stories were received in English.

I first went to the Hopi Reservation during the summer of 1971, after having taken fieldwork technique courses at Indiana University with Richard M. Dorson, Harold E. Driver, and George List. At that time, I intended to study the music of Hopi dance ceremonies, because Harry C. James had encouraged me to do so. Mr. James had spent a number of years at the various Hopi villages and told me often of his love for the Hopi people. I soon discovered that I was able to do little more than talk *about* the music, since the Hopi people place severe restrictions on the tape recording of certain kinds of music and certain occasions. I continued to go back once or twice each year for twelve years. Each time, I took extensive notes on the villages, the demeanor of the people, and the various public ceremonies that I attended there.

Along the way, I had the good fortune to meet and develop a deep friendship with W. L. Satewa, who lives at First Mesa, in the village of Sichomovi (Place of the Flowers). I learned many good stories from Mr. Satewa.

Before meeting Mr. Satewa, I had studied folklore at Indiana University, and I had informally collected oral narratives from my friends, relatives, and other students regularly since 1971. The Hopi stories excited my imagination like no others. Unlike the restrictions with music, fewer barriers appeared in story collecting, for the Hopi people shared their stories far more willingly than they shared their music.

Hopi stories are abundant. Both men and women tell them—in the home, where television sometimes competes with them, and in the kiva, or on ceremonial occasions. During 1982, I collected the seven stories of this project. Mr. Satewa told me "The Coyote and the Beaver," "The Coyote and the Turtle," "A Witchcraft Story," and "The Coyote and the Black Snake" in English. Another Hopi and two non-Indians were present. An eighty-year-old storyteller told "Poowak Wuhti," "Hano Wuhti," and "Awatovi Story" to Mr. Satewa and me in

Hopi. Each of the stories was told while my tape recorder was turned on. Other members of the storyteller's family were present at the narration of these stories. Mr. Satewa had told me that this old person "had" these stories. Hopi people always say, "I *have* a story," never "I *know* a story," even those who fully command idiomatic English. Such a practice suggests possession, rather than merely knowledge. Each time I received a story, I gave some money in exchange. Neither storyteller "sold" a story. A business transaction, in the non-Indian sense, did not take place; we exchanged gifts.

My first difficult task was to listen repeatedly to the tape recording of each story and transcribe the text onto paper with the typewriter. Mr. Satewa requested numerous revisions. At each stage of revision, Mr. Satewa read the text, and I proceeded no further until he approved each revision. He listened repeatedly to the tape recordings of the three Hopi language stories and translated them into English, directly onto another tape, with the use of a second recorder. When he was satisfied that his translation of each story was accurate, I then followed the same procedure as with the other stories.

Writing Hopi presents problems. Even today, spelling varies considerably. The Hopi Reservation community schools currently are attempting to standardize spelling, but as yet no complete dictionary exists, although many little dictionaries and word lists are available. The First Mesa schools sponsored an essay and creative writing contest in 1981. The following rules for writing appeared in the Hopi newspaper:

> Essays may be written on any subject, either in English or in Hopi. Creative writing must be in Hopi.
>
> Essays will be judged on originality, spelling, punctuation, and grammar (in English); or originality, consistency of spelling, and grammar (in Hopi).
>
> Creative writing will be judged on originality, consistency of spelling, and grammar.[1]

In written Hopi, "consistency of spelling" seems to satisfy the Hopi people at this time. Although many words have become nearly standardized by virtue of their frequent use in the media, novel spellings appear with regularity. At present, the method of writing Hopi that is sanctioned by the University of Arizona, at least for scholarly work, is the one developed by Ekkehart Malotki. In this book only names and brief expressions appear in Hopi.

So far as I have been able to discover, no one has acknowledged in scholarly research that there may not be a single Hopi dialect, but two, or possibly three. Each mesa has its own terms and names for many things, and pronunciation varies from mesa to mesa. Pitch inflection, for example, is a characteristic of Third Mesa speech patterns. I notice occa-

sional rising and falling pitch differentiation in First Mesa speech also. Whether a more complex inflection system was ever a characteristic of First Mesa is impossible to determine without further comparative studies. If it was, it has undergone pejoration. First Mesa Hopis smile at what they call the "sing-song" speech of those at Oraibi (Third Mesa), much as Midwest and Coastal non-Indians smile at speech patterns of the Deep South.

1. *Qua' Toqti,* 5 March 1981, 2.

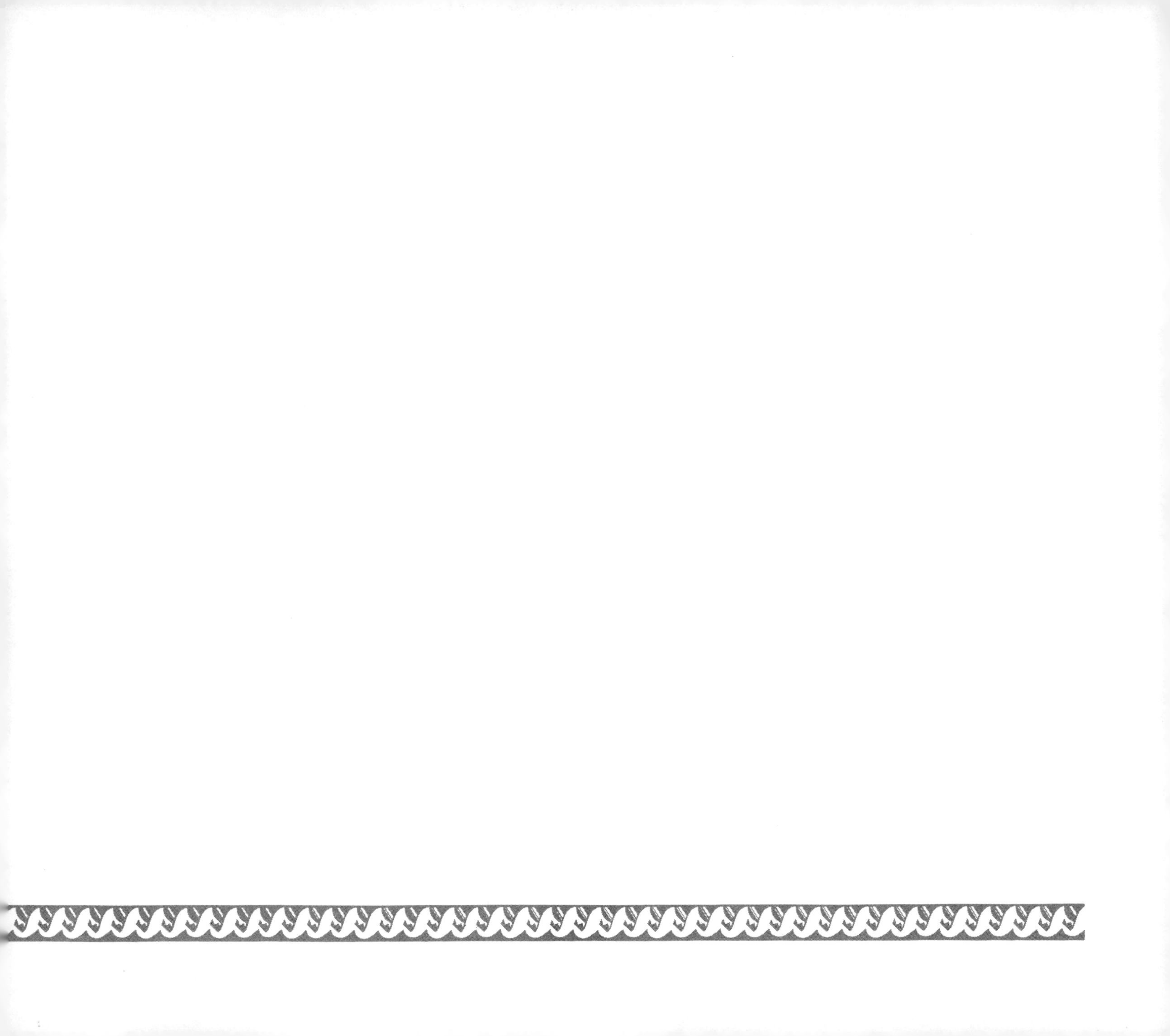

W. L. Satewa

WL was born 19 August 1937 at Keams Canyon, Arizona, on the Hopi Reservation. At the age of three, he moved with his parents to Sichomovi, or Middle Village, on First Mesa. His mother belongs to the Butterfly Clan, and his father belongs to the Flute Clan. At the appropriate age of twelve, he was initiated into the kiva fraternity, as most young Hopi boys are, in order to gain knowledge of the kachina fraternity. He was initiated into a Hopi fraternity in Tewa Village, having chosen a Tewa to be his ceremonial father. Mr. Satewa's kiva is located in the village of Hano (also called Tewa), the easternmost village of First Mesa. Since all villages of First Mesa function as a unit in maintaining the annual ceremonial cycle, Mr. Satewa attends or assists in the various ceremonies of all the villages to some degree. He is a regular participant in the ceremonies of his own fraternity, which, he says, correspond to the Hopi *Soyala* fraternity. After his tour of service in the marines, he returned to the reservation and was initiated into the knowledge of the Blue Flute Fraternity at Walpi Village.

Mr. Satewa embraces the Hopi Way, a way of life which makes no distinction between sacred and secular in the European sense. The Hopi Way permeates virtually all aspects of Hopi existence. He expresses concern with preserving the Hopi traditions and with passing on "the old stories" to the young, particularly to his own natural and ceremonial children. (Children who are to be initiated into a fraternity choose a ceremonial "father," one outside the nuclear family and one knowledgeable in the fraternity into which they will be initiated.) Being Hopi by birth and Tewa and Hopi by ceremonial affiliation, Mr. Satewa has a broad spectrum of knowledge of First Mesa traditions as well as regular contact with the daily life of the villages. Being a well-respected member of his community, he sometimes is chosen for a role of honor in the winter kachina ceremonies. I have spent a good deal of time with Mr. Satewa, with his mother and father in their home, and in the homes and villages of other relatives; I clearly see that he is both loved and esteemed.

Mr. Satewa is an artist, both in temperament and in skill.

He earns money by selling traditionally carved and painted kachina dolls. At home, he sells a few dolls to tourists. He sells, however, in greater quantity while traveling throughout the country with Indian art shows. Having a traditional viewpoint, he refuses to carve certain kachina dolls for commercial purposes because he considers them to be too sacred. (Within the Hopi religion, certain kachinas may not be viewed by the public.) In addition to carving, he has mastered the arts of weaving, jewelry making, and storytelling.

Mr. Satewa is in contact with the old people who know "the old stories" and is a responsible Hopi father, both natural and ceremonial, who passes on the stories to the young. He has lived off the reservation for short periods of time, having a sister who lives in the Los Angeles, California, area. Because of his business dealings, he has traveled and met many people, both Indian and non-Indian. Exposure created by his military tour of duty and the fact that he is a fairly avid reader have given him a broad world view.

As a carrier of traditional oral literature, Mr. Satewa is an ideal storyteller. He speaks Hopi and English fluently, as well as some Tewa. As a teacher's aide in the Hopi schools, he was exposed in a professional way to the peculiarities of bilingualism. While working on this project, he usually outguessed my likely problems with Hopi sounds.

I personally have encouraged Mr. Satewa to record, either on tape or in writing, the traditional stories of his people so that they will not be lost. He is amenable to this suggestion, since he is aware that already many of the stories are completely lost or imperfectly remembered. Such a task of recording is not easy, for many of the older Hopi people fear that their stories will be taken and used in an impious manner. The Hopi stories are comparable to the parables in the Bible, and in both the Indian and non-Indian sense, they are sacred "scripture." Since the Hopi people remain sensitive to the fact that outsiders have not always fully respected their land, art, religion, and customs, I hope that those who read these stories will afford them the same kind of respect they give other works of literature.

Acknowledgments

I wish to thank my good friend WL for sharing his stories. I am grateful for his unrelenting concern to "get them right," both in English and in writing. Special acknowledgment is due to WL's family: his mother, his father, his brother, and all of WL's children, who explained and clarified much of the Hopi Way, while sharing their home and food with me on numerous occasions.

I wish to thank Helen Jaskoski, who patiently read my drafts, offered helpful suggestions, and encouraged me. She is a thorough-going scholar whose assistance I deeply appreciate. I gratefully acknowledge the assistance of Alice-Lyle Scoufos,

Jane Hipolito, Dwight Lomayesva, and Vincent Standing-Deer Gomez for their encouragement and interest in the project. I wish to give special thanks to Margery Thomason, who frequently "bounced ideas" back and forth with me. And finally, I wish to thank all the Hopi people, named and unnamed, who were so kind and helpful to me.

Introduction

The Hopi Indians live on a reservation in the northeastern corner of Arizona. Today a dozen Hopi villages string in an east-to-west direction over a distance of some seventy-five miles.

Hano Village on First Mesa, the only village that is not Hopi, was settled by people from the Rio Grande area about the beginning of the eighteenth century. Some of the settlements that were established by other incoming groups have disappeared, though some of their ruins remain.[1] Hano Village, also called Tewa, shares the top of First Mesa (or East Mesa) with Sichomovi and Walpi. Below the mesa is a village called Polacca. On Second Mesa, to the west, are Shongopovi, Mishongnovi, and Shipaulovi. Old Oraibi is on the Third

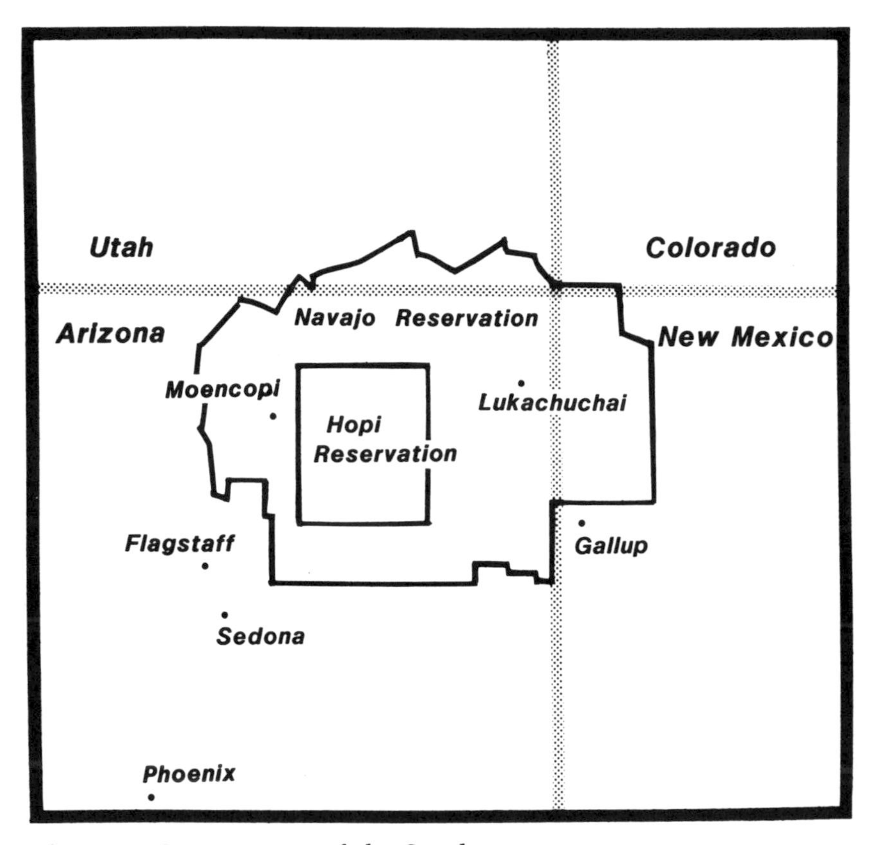

The Four Corners area of the Southwest
showing the location of the Hopi Reservation

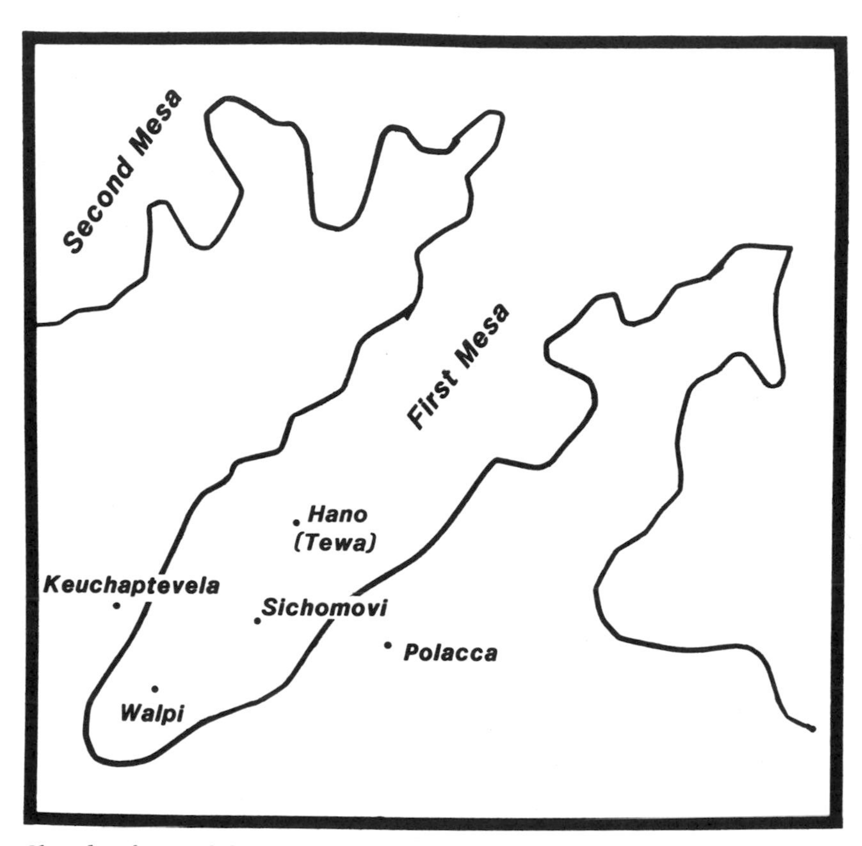

Sketch of First Mesa

Mesa a few miles farther west, with Kykotsmovi (also called New Oraibi) below the mesa on the east side. Sharing the mesa top are Hotevilla and Bacavi. Some fifty miles farther west, near Tuba City, is the village of Moencopi, often referred to as the twin villages of Upper and Lower Moencopi. The Hopis call Moencopi "the Hopi Island," since it is separated from the Hopi Reservation "mainland."

The Navajo Reservation completely surrounds the Hopi Reservation, and according to Mr. Satewa, "We are brothers." The Hopis and the Navajos, however, have not been the best of relatives, having had disagreements over land use, both today and in the past. Don Talayesva, speaking of his young boyhood at the turn of the century said, "We Hopis hated the Navahos."[2] Today, with so much interaction between so many Indian groups and non-Indians, "What are loosely referred to as 'Hopi traditions,' therefore, is a collection of traditions brought by numerous groups from a variety of places."[3]

The First Mesa Tewas have retained what they regard as a distinct identity through preservation of their language and traditions, even while absorbing Hopi mainstream culture. The Tewa situation as it related to the Hopi mainstream is somewhat comparable to that of other ethnic minorities as they relate to American mainstream life. The Tewa speak Hopi as well as Tewa; they mingle and intermarry with Hopis, and they share Hopi ceremonies and life in general. At the same time, they tenaciously hold on to their Tewa identity as best they can. Their retention of their particular traditions is paralleled by each Hopi clan's nurturing of its own history, legends, beliefs, and accomplishments.

Today all the villages still retain a set of pre-conquest officials. Each village has a number of religious organizations, comparable to non-Indian churches, lodges, fraternities, and faith-healing groups. Each "chapter" of each type of religious society has its own officers who decide the fate of citizens accused of such crimes as witchcraft or betrayal of religious secrets, including the telling of tales to outsiders.[4]

According to Mr. Satewa, this power of the officials is no longer exercised as it was in the past. Because of this tradition, however, most Hopis are reluctant to tell tales, legends, myths, and other stories, all of which are religious in the Indian sense, to non-Hopis. Those who do frequently refuse to allow their name to be published. For this reason, the teller of "Poowak Wuhti," "Hano Wuhti," and "Awatovi Story" remains anonymous in this collection. The storyteller is an eighty-year-old descendant of the Hano people who now reside in the Hano Village.

In general, when I use the word, "Hopi," I include the people, stories, and ceremonials of Hano (Tewa Village), since the amount of acculturation between the Hopis and the First Mesa Tewas over the last three hundred years or so has been considerable. The first three stories of this collection are specifically Hopi, although as suggested in the biography of W. L.

Satewa, the storyteller, there is the likelihood of Tewa influence.

Language. For the translation of the three Hopi language stories, I relied almost entirely on Mr. Satewa; with his approval, I sometimes rephrased portions of the text. We aimed for consistency in spelling, and we used the more or less standard spelling of place names. We attempted neither a totally free translation of the Hopi, nor a literal translation. We did lean toward an approximation of the sense of the original Hopi, giving weight to readability in English.

History. The Hopi people are believed to be the descendants of the Anasazi, Mogollon, and Hohokam, prehistoric groups who migrated to the Hopi mesas in Arizona. In the 1500s, the ancestors of the present-day Hopi lived in settlements scattered along the Rio Grande and its tributaries. The Zuni and Hopi situated their pueblos on high, protective mesas in western New Mexico and eastern Arizona. They were farmers; their principal crop was corn, although they also produced beans, squash, and tobacco. The environment was like a desert, rarely receiving more than ten inches of rainfall each year. The early Pueblo people overcame this problem of aridity by constructing irrigation works along the Rio Grande and its tributaries, by developing varieties of corn that would withstand intense heat and drought, and by focusing their religious attention upon those supernatural forces that they believed controlled nature's rainmaking apparatus.[5]

Spanish settlements pushed their way into the Southwest. By the 1680s, Jesuits had established a chain of missions under the leadership of Father Kino. As carrier of Spanish civilization, Kino worked to convert the peoples in their scattered agricultural settlements. In 1695, the pueblos revolted, killed missionaries, burned public buildings, and drove off livestock.[6] According to Harry C. James, "From Taos to Zuni, everything Spanish that the victorious Indians could find was destroyed."[7] Mr. James gives an account of this period of Hopi history, from which the following is a summary. The exact date when the rebellion began on the Hopi mesas is not known, but we do know that Catholic priests were killed at both the villages of Awatovi (now a ruin) and Shongopovi, and the mission churches were destroyed. The ruins are still visible today. One of the chief reasons for the revolt of the Hopi is that the priests made slaves of the Hopis, forcing them to carry logs over many miles to build the mission churches. A number of attempts at reconquest were made by the Spanish, but none was successful.

The Hopi continued to be subject to a number of invaders: the raiding bands of Navajos, the Mormon church, and practically every other denomination since the British colonial period in eastern North America. In 1923, Commissioner of Indian Affairs Charles H. Burke attempted to abolish all forms of Indian religion. The Indian Bureau "sent out men to gather information designed to make out that Indian religions were 'pornographic in the extreme.'"[8] Such intrusions by outside groups have caused the Hopi people to close their religious ceremonies to non-Hopis, a practice which is still carried out today in all villages to some degree.

Theology and the Ceremonial Cycle. According to tradition, corn is the Mother of the Hopi people. Without corn, there is no food. In a land where rainfall is scant and harsh weather the norm, the Hopi feel a need for supernatural assistance to insure that corn will grow. I know no Hopi who denies the necessity of cooperation with the supernatural in order to insure good crops. "Long ago," says Barton Wright, former scientific director of the Museum of Man in San Diego, "this need was formalized in its presentation, reinforced by similar rites of other Pueblo people, and compounded into a bewildering complexity of ceremonies, rituals, and interacting groups."[9] Mr. Satewa agrees that Wright's statements are probably true. Bewildering and complex are key words in describing the ceremonial cycle of the Hopi. Although there is a conviction among the Hopi that each person contributes his part to the cooperative prayer dances of the yearly cycle, no single individual knows all the prayers and dances that are performed in the dozen villages of Hopiland. Each village has its own rituals, and each kiva fraternity has its own secret rites that are not shared with any other group. No question exists, however, that cooperation is a core value of the Hopis: the husband and wife each have their prayers and rituals at the household level;

each kiva fraternity has its part at the village level; and each village has its part at the mesa level.

Hopi theology and ritual participation are explained in Barton Wright's "Hopi Ritual":

> Hopi ceremonial life is interwoven by the belief that nature and God are one and that the universe is totally reliable if properly approached. Every object possesses a spirit or animus of its own which can be coerced to intercede for the Hopi in his dual world of the natural and the supernatural. . . . The important forces of this universe are given living form and are called kachinas. . . . Kachinas are rain-bearing spirits given visual form by the Hopi men through paint and costume. It is believed that when the men don masks, they become the spirit or kachina and that with the proper song, and dance they can produce tangible benefits.[10]

Mr. Satewa concurs with this explanation.

The yearly cycle is divided into two more or less equal halves. The two halves (roughly divided by December and June), reflect the dualities—winter-summer, night-day, metaphysical-physical—and complementary ceremonies are performed in each half. Beginning at the winter solstice, the kachinas come to the villages. Events and time periods vary slightly among the three mesas. At summer solstice, the kachinas "go home." That is, they go into the metaphysical realm. The spiritual realm is given a tangible location, the San Francisco Peaks, near Flagstaff, Arizona.

Most of the ceremonies and some of the kachina dances occur inside the kiva, a semi-subterranean ceremonial house. Public ceremonies take place in the dancing plaza of each village. The summer solstice begins the non-kachina dances, the so-called social dances. The winter solstice dances are the start of the kachina season. The kachina season is marked by the return of a single kachina who appears from outside the village to "open" the kiva and allow the "return" of the other kachinas. All dances follow a fairly set form, regardless of whether they are kachina or unmasked social dances. A line of dancers moves into the rectangular space of the plaza and dances on each of the four sides.

The dances, prayers, songs, and stories are each a part of what Hopis call the Hopi Way and what non-Hopis call Hopi religion or theology. Hopi teaching stories contain principles of the Hopi Way, and the Hopi people tell certain ones during particular seasons and on certain occasions. An "old story" is sacred and must not be treated carelessly. Careless treatment includes telling a story during the wrong season. *Kyamuya,* which corresponds generally with the month of December, is the storytelling month. Traditionally, Hopis upheld a summer taboo. "Whoever tells a story in the summertime will be bitten by the rattlesnake," according to Mr. Satewa. "The Hopi people believed that stories should be told only in the winter season; to tell them at any other time was wrong. If a person did tell a story out of season, a snake bite was his punishment." Mr. Satewa goes on to say that, "A storyteller is safe during the cold season as long as the ground is frozen, since cold-blooded snakes cannot move fast enough to strike." Today, some storytellers recite this summer taboo, often adding, "That's the way it was in the old days," but few actually observe it now. I received the narratives in this presentation outside the kiva, at various times during the year.

Much traditional Hopi literature, through lack of written record, has been lost. Earlier I indicated that stories are abundant and that storytelling remains a thriving part of Hopi life. Some explanation is needed. While storytelling continues and stories are numerous, certain stories have been lost or imperfectly remembered. Mr. Satewa, for example, could find no one able to piece together fragments of a story he had heard as a boy. What survives is impressive and vital to the body of world literature. Much of the literature has not been accessible because the Hopi people have not wished to share it with others. At present, however, a few foresighted Hopis wish to preserve the literature from extinction by having it recorded in print. The stories of this collection are examples of living literature of First Mesa; they continue to be told.

1. Albert Yava and Harold Courlander, *Big Falling Snow: A Tewa-Hopi Indian's Life and Times and the History and Traditions of His People* (New York: Crown Publishers, Inc., 1978), vii.

2. Leo W. Simmons and Don Talayesva, *Sun Chief: The Autobiography of a Hopi Indian* (New Haven: Yale University Press, 1963), 107.

3. Yava and Courlander, vii.

4. Harold E. Driver, *Indians of North America* (Chicago: The University of Chicago Press, 1961), 296.

5. Arrell Morgan Gibson, *The American Indian: Prehistory to the Present* (Lexington: D. C. Heath and Company, 1980), 73.

6. Ibid., 105.

7. Harry C. James, *Pages from Hopi History* (Tucson: The University of Arizona Press, 1979), 54.

8. Ibid., 188.

9. Tyrone Stewart, et al., *The Year of the Hopi* (Washington, D. C.: Smithsonian Institution Traveling Exhibition Service, 1981), 17.

10. Ibid., 17.

The Coyote and the Beaver

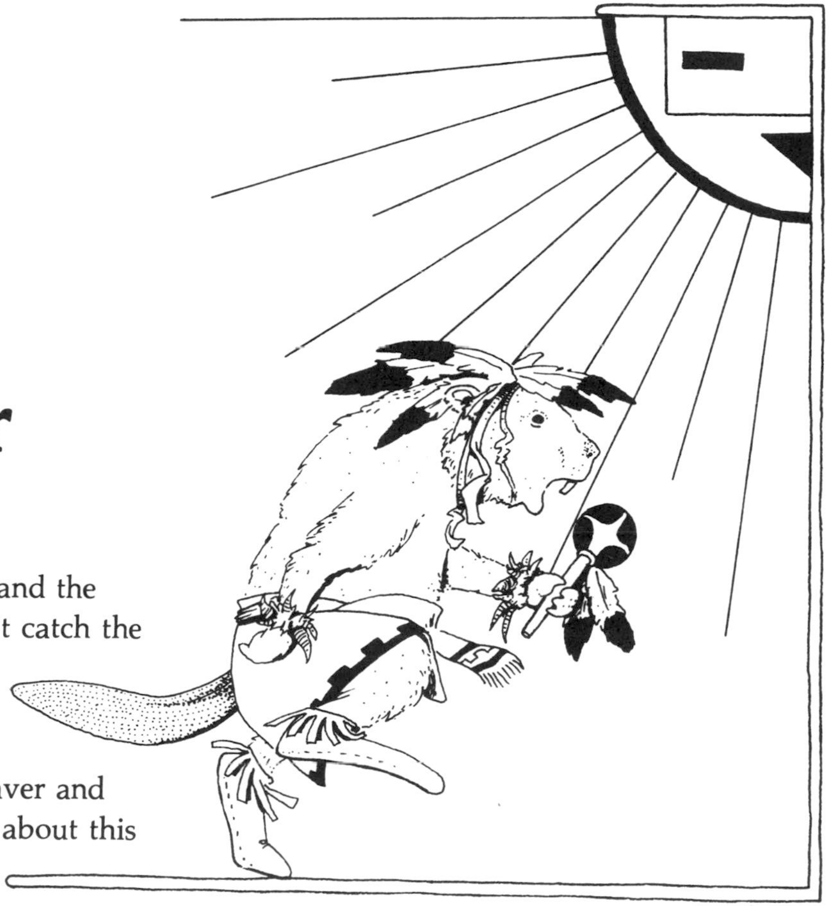

This is a teaching story. It's about Coyote and the Beaver. Coyote was getting old and couldn't catch the game he was after. On a hot day of poor hunting, he became thirsty and decided to go for a drink. He came upon a pond where a beaver family was living. Beaver and Coyote made friends and talked and talked about this and that until Beaver finally asked Coyote if he were hungry.

Coyote answered shyly, "Yes, I'm hungry." Then more humbly. "I'll eat anything you have to offer."

He sang a magic chant and said powerful magic words.

Beaver then replied, "Are you sure you will eat anything I offer you?"

"Yes," answered Coyote.

So Beaver invited Coyote saying, "Well, then, let's go over to my house and have something to eat." They went to Beaver's house and smoked the pipe and talked and exchanged news of their surroundings.

Shortly after mid-day, Beaver said he would get the dinner food ready. As Coyote watched, beaver called his children to come home. As each little beaver came through the opening to the house, Papa beaver caught him by the legs and hit him over the head and killed him. Then he skinned and cleaned them and put them in a pot of boiling water to cook.

By now, Coyote wasn't sure whether he wanted to eat there. But he did promise and so he decided to honor that promise. By late afternoon, the food was cooked and Beaver set down eating bowls for each of them, and they began their meal. Coyote, tasting cautiously at first and finding the stew very good, began to eat in earnest. He never tasted anything as good.

Beaver kept his eyes alert, and each time one of them would finish eating a carcass, he would pick up the bones and wrap them in the skins of the little beavers. Each one was kept separate. Coyote wasn't aware of Beaver doing this. When they had eaten all of the little beavers, they moved away from the eating area and smoked and talked some more until Coyote mentioned that he must be on his way.

After Coyote departed, Beaver took the small bundles of skin and bones and went to the water's edge. He sang a magic chant and said powerful magic words and tossed the small bundles of skin and bones into the water. When the little bundles hit the water, they turned back into live little beavers again, playing and laughing in the water.

Sometime later, Coyote was hunting in the vicinity of the beaver home and decided to go have a drink at the pond and see if his beaver friend still lived in the area. He got to the water, had his drink and found Beaver in the same place. He noticed Beaver's children playing in the water. They appeared to be a little larger than the last time he was here, and Coyote couldn't figure that out, because he remembered that he and Beaver had eaten them last time.

Coyote and Beaver talked and exchanged news until beaver finally asked how hunting was. Coyote said, "I get a rabbit here and there, sometimes a squirrel or prairie dog, but they're scarce these days." Then Beaver noticed Coyote's rib cage and how poorly he looked and said, "Why don't you come over to my house and eat with me, you've eaten there before."

Coyote thought about the last time, but decided that a meal was hard to turn down. So he accepted and followed Beaver home.

Beaver went through the same thing that he did before, calling the children, killing them, and skinning and boiling

them in a cooking pot. Coyote was all eyes and ears this time. He watched everything that was going on, because he suddenly realized or sensed that something magical was taking place.

After eating, they sat together and smoked and made small talk. Coyote finally told Beaver he would be on his way home. But he didn't go home. Instead, he hid in the brush near the pond where he could keep an eye on the beaver house and the pond. He saw the beaver go through his ritual and make the children come back to life. He also learned the chant and magic words which were really very simple. He slinked away from the pond and got out into the open country, then ran like the wind toward home. He was just dying to try out the magic spell. "I've got the secret, I've just got to try it," he thought to himself.

He arrived home and called his children and killed them. Then he skinned and cooked them in boiling water, just like Beaver had done. Then he invited all his relatives to come and share his meal.

When all was eaten and the guests had left, Coyote, singing happily because he knew he was going to get his children back, went to a nearby pond. He then went through the chant and song ritual and threw the bones and skins into the water. Due to the magic in the chant and the words, the children *did* come back to life, but Coyote was shocked to see that all of his children were deformed! Some had two heads, others had six tails, others one leg; and others had none of these, for Coyote had missed the main ingredient: keeping the bones of each carcass *separate.* Instead, he had jumbled them all up into one big pile and had thrown them into the water like that, and that is what caused the deformations.

Coyote cried and cried over his children, and this is why you should never try to do things you know nothing about. Especially in magic or witchcraft.

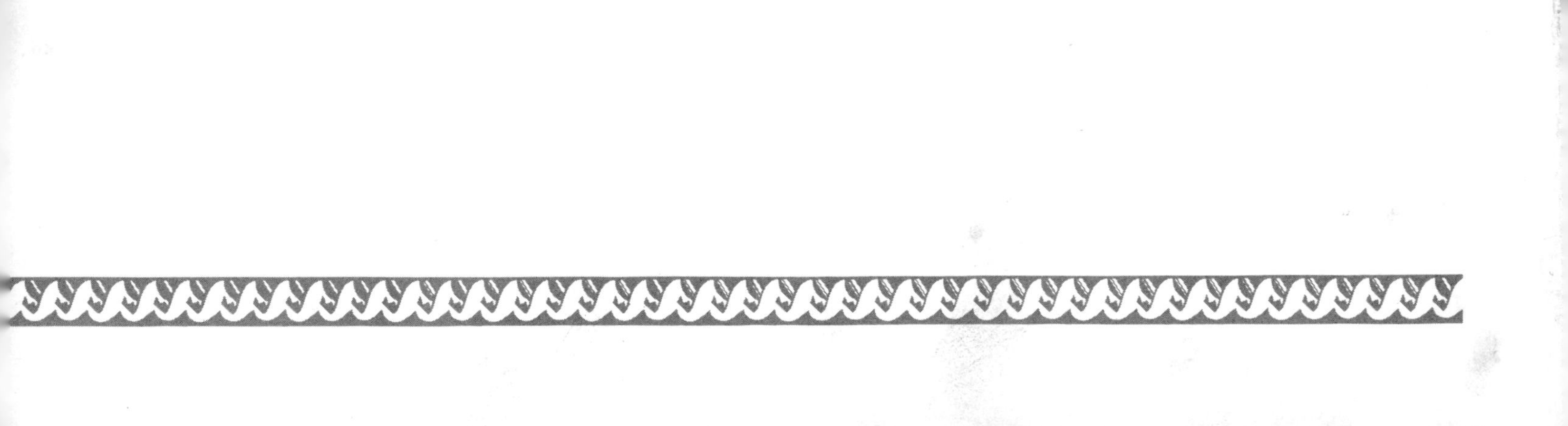

The Coyote and the Turtle

This is a teaching story. It's about the coyote and the turtle. There was a coyote that reached old age, and his hunting abilities weren't what they used to be. He had trouble catching game and things to keep him fed. It finally came to where he could only get small things like muskrat, things that were slower than he was, slow rabbits, and things like that.

One day he was hunting along running water, or a stream; it could be the Sedona area. Some place where there are a lot of slippery stones near the water. And he happened to run across a turtle. He made friends with him, and he was talking with

And when they got there, they went through the top, down through the ladder, kiva-style.

him, and the turtle said, "I can tell by looking at you; you're not filled out." Then he asked, "Would you like to share a meal with me?"

And the Coyote said, "Sure, I'll share a meal with you."

So the turtle took him to his home. And when they got there, they went through the top, down through the ladder, kiva-style.

The coyote, even before he got to the kiva, could smell meat boiling, and he wondered what kind it was. When he got there. . . . It's not the custom to ask any direct questions. When you're invited to a place, your presence and good manners are what is required, not all kinds of questions. So he never questioned him.

Finally Turtle brought out a pottery of stew, a bowl, and so— they ate. They ate well. Coyote really "dug in." It was really good, he thought, but he couldn't figure out what it was. He was thinking, "Rabbit?" He thought things like, "Rabbit? It's not muskrat."

After the meal, they sat together. But he couldn't get the question of meat out of his mind. So they sat, and they smoked pipes. Smoke to us in the Hopi Way brings relaxation. We smoke pipes, even before prayers. Before you pray, you smoke to relax, get your thoughts together. And so after they smoked, they both felt relaxed, and Coyote knew that now was the time to ask the question. So he said, "That meat we had today, it was really, really good, but I couldn't place what it was, what kind of meat it was. And it was so plentiful that I just wondered how a little hunter like you could get such meat?"

The turtle looked at him and studied him for a while. He thought he was serious enough, so he started giving him correct answers. "That was deer meat," he said.

The coyote started laughing, you know. Right away he said, "No little turtle like you could get deer meat." Then he caught himself. He said to himself, "I wonder if it *is* deer meat, because the turtle never cracked or moved or anything. He just kept his eye on me to see what my reaction would be." And then he asked the turtle, "Well, how did you get it?"

The turtle said, "That is a secret of mine that I can't give out right now. But whenever you come back to this area, stop by," he said, "and I'll have my deer meat."

So they departed. And many months passed. Coyote was hunting alone, and he couldn't get any more game. Then he remembered the turtle. "I'll go check on that guy and see if he really has something." And he went back to the turtle's kiva and hollered in: "No! Ying ya ai."

The turtle answered, so he went down the ladder. "So, it's you again, my friend," the turtle said to the coyote.

"Yeah," Coyote answered, "I was just in the area, and I thought I would stop by," he said.

"Are you hungry?" Turtle asked.

"No, not really, but I thought I'd visit you while I'm here," Coyote lied.

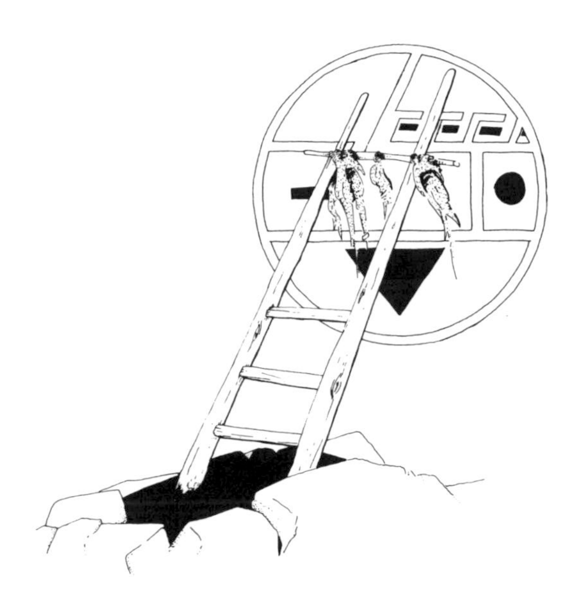

The turtle said, "Well, I'll feed you anyway," he said. So he went into the back room of his kiva and came back out with a pottery bowl of steaming meat, just as before. The coyote and the turtle ate and then smoked.

And then the coyote asked him again the question of how he got his meat. And the turtle told him. He said, "I told you before: that is a secret of mine. The last time you asked me what the meat was, I didn't tell you then, but this time I know you're not laughing," he said.

Then the coyote asked him: "Is it really deer meat? You get a whole deer?"

Turtle said, "Yes."

Coyote asked, "You don't steal from somebody or have friends who kill them for you?"

Turtle said, "No, I get my own game."

Coyote asked him, "Well, will you teach me how to do it?"

Turtle answered, "I will teach you if you promise to keep it a secret, something that is a secret between you and me. And you can't pass it out to any of your coyote friends, or relatives—wolves, fox, dogs, and so on. And you have to make that a true promise."

So the coyote promised. And Turtle said, "I'll show you in four days. We'll make preparations."

So the first day they got their gear together—knife, spear, rope—things they were going to use. Second day, their paints. Third day, their feathers. The fourth day, they were ready.

They tied their prayer feathers early and said their prayers.

They went to the stream; Turtle went first, and Coyote followed. Coyote kept his eye on what was happening. He noticed that the turtle was watching for tracks along the edge of the stream. And when he found a place where there were plentiful tracks, he knew that that was the place where the deer would come to drink.

Turtle said, "This is it," he said; "now we'll have to wait 'til the sun gets down a little further. Now we've found what we're looking for. Now we'll go out and get ourselves ready."

So they went out into the trees there, a little forest of jack pines, and made their prayers and their prayer feathers. Prayers are always offered, you know, when it's time to kill: "My brother, I have to take your life to feed myself and my children and my children's children." This is always the prayer offered to the animal you're after. So they said their prayers and put on their red *su' ta.* (I don't know the translation of *su' ta*; that's their hunter's eyemark, you know. When they're hunting, the *su' ta* shades the eyes and cuts down the glare.)

Then he went back to where the tracks were. It was near the time so. . . . The story I'm telling you, this is a legend, and is about a time, you know, when everybody walked as humans and could change their form. So Turtle went back to the water there, and they got ready. He posted the coyote a distance away. He said, "I don't want your smell near."

Then they went into the water and bathed; both of them

bathed. Turtle said, "The coyote always has a distinctive smell, so you go on the other side of the stream because I know they're going to come from this side. So you get up on that high bluff there, and you watch. Disguise yourself carefully and watch."

So the coyote went across to the bluff, and the turtle got ready. He put his bow and arrows away and got his spears out and stuck them in the ground with the points up. He stuck them on both sides of where he was. And then, since he had taken his bath already and was still wet, he got some clay—a clay mixture that runs in certain parts near the water; he got some of that slippery clay and spread it all over his shell, all over the back of his shell. Then he lay down at the water's edge and made himself, you know, the size of a normal turtle.

And toward evening, it was about dusk, you could hear the branches breaking. That's when he got himself settled, really settled. Before, he was just waiting; now he settled himself and pulled himself inside his shell. His feet were braced solidly, and they were disguised by the clay. He was on a solid-rock place.

Then here come the deer. They came one by one. Looked around. They didn't see anything that was unfamiliar. Everything looked the same as usual. So then they trotted on down toward the water, and they looked again. No sign of anything. So the leader of the group, a big buck, came and started to drink, and he stepped on the turtle shell. And when the turtle felt him, he got ready. He started flexing his muscles.

And then when the deer started to drink—when he put his head down and was off balance—Turtle jerked himself out from under the hoof. When he did that, the deer lost his balance and fell on the sharpened spear. When that happened, all the other deer ran away. The turtle jumped up, turned himself back into an almost-human form, and he caught his deer. The coyote watched all this happen. Then he came and helped take the meat home.

A few days later, the coyote wanted to try it. So he went to his own kiva. Got his ritual gear. Made his preparations. Made everything as right as possible. Made his sticks. Then he went up and down the stream. He said, "I'm not going to use the same place that belongs to Turtle. My first one will be of my own choosing."

So he went through the same ritual. He found tracks, and then he got ready. It was almost getting to be dark then. He made his prayer about "My Brother, I need to kill you to feed myself," and he put on his *su' ta.* He went to the edge of the water, waited there, and waited there.

"Nothing seems to be coming." These were his thoughts. He was just about ready to give up when he heard the branches breaking. He dug himself deeper into the mud there. His clay was kind of dried a little bit on his back, so he sprinkled some more water on the clay. And then he waited some more. Then he heard the deer coming closer. He knew they were coming. He looked at his pointed sticks on both sides of him. "I wonder which one of these sticks will get him? Which way should I jump? Which one will I be able to catch first," he thought?

The first one that came out was the leader of that little herd. It was a big one. Bigger than the other one that they had gotten earlier. He could tell because when it walked, he could feel it stamping hard. The deer got to the edge of the water and looked both ways, and then started to feel his way closer. He got to where the coyote was lying. He started to go there for a drink. It was a little bit shallow there. He slipped and missed his step and then quickly stepped with the other foot. When he did, he stepped right on Coyote's back. So instead of the coyote getting the deer, the deer got the coyote. His hoof went through the back of the coyote, and so the coyote was done for.

So they tell us—the old folks—the moral of the story is, "Never try to be somebody you aren't. Or something you're not. Only be yourself."

That's the story of the coyote and the turtle.

The Coyote and the Black Snake

. . . Coyote told him about a big black snake that would come by "Homolovi"

According to Mr. Satewa, who heard "The Coyote and the Black Snake" in the kiva, this story is a "modern myth."

Jarold Ramsey retells an anecdote that is very pertinent to "modern myths." The story goes that somewhere in the Southwest a few years ago, a young ethnographer ran into an old storyteller, who after much attention and favors, agreed to recite some stories on tape for the young man. The old lady enjoyed the young man's company so much that when she came to the end of her narrative, she went right on, unknown to him, inventing her content in the traditional style. When the ethnographer, back in his study, realized what his informant had done, he erased the nontraditional tapes in a scholarly fury. Ramsey argues, and most all would agree, that it was precisely the moment when the old storyteller began to invent, borrow, and adapt material for her narrative that the ethnographer ought to have been most alert and curious. He might have been studying mythology-in-progress (Ramsey, 168). We have such a rare opportunity with the "The Coyote and the Black Snake."

"I tuwutsi. Yaw hisat yeesiwa." This is a story about Coyote and the Big Black Snake. There lived a coyote on the north side of Polacca, along the Wepo Wash. And he'd go out hunting, up and down the Wash, through Sheep Springs and Wepo. And he'd meet other coyotes. And one day, he met a fellow coyote, and the coyote told him about a big black snake that would come by "Homolovi," about sixty-five miles south of Polacca. It would make stops in "Pahivi." They don't know what it does, but it makes a lot of noise, screeches, and crunches. And then it will go on.

Then Coyote, with his curiosity, decided that he would make a trip to "Homolovi," to see this big black snake. So he left Wepo Wash, crossed through the Gap of First Mesa, went down the other side, and headed south toward Badger Butte. He continued on, and he passed "Piitakwi," or Breast Butte. And he saw the next butte, and he knew that there was water there. This is called "Yatqo̲ tukwi." And he got to

"Yatqo̲ tukwi," or Saddle Butte, and he found a spring, and drank, and rested. And then he continued on south until he got to "Mo̲no̲qu tukwi," or The Butte with the Baby Antelope Necklace. This is a mound with a ring of baby antelope around it. Where the antelope mothers drop their offspring. And there he found water again. He drank there, and then he cut across, through the Little Painted Desert, and he got to the flats. Then he ran the rest of the way to "Homolovi."

He got to "Homolovi," and he topped the rise, and he waited around, out of sight of the village there. Soon he heard something coming. And so he hid behind the brush and some rocks and waited, and along comes the big black snake. He's watching it. And the snake comes along, making all kinds of noise. Rattling along. And he could hear it snapping his teeth. Just going, "Snap-snappity-snap-snap, snap-snappity-snap-snap." And it was breathing fire from its head. And he could see the smoke coming out of the head.

And the big black snake went on curving its way, and it goes to "Pahivi," or Winslow. And then Coyote could hear the snake screeching, and he wondered what it was. But he was afraid of it, and afraid to go check. So he stayed there and watched the snake come and go. Each time he would try to see what it was really doing. And he noticed that it just kept going along its path and didn't bother anything. So he moved up closer.

Then one day, he noticed some cows and cattle in the area

where the snake usually comes through. And he said "Uh-huh, now this big black snake is going to get one of those cows. This, I gotta see." And so he moves up closer and watches. And the snake comes along breathing fire and smoke from his head. "He doesn't bother the cattle!" And the coyote was disappointed, and he said, "What's the matter with that big snake? What does he eat anyway?"

And then the snake goes on into "Pahivi," and he stops, making all these noises, these crunching noises. And Coyote says, "Maybe he eats metal, or wood, or something else we're not used to seeing a big black snake eat." So he decides to get up closer, so he can see the big black snake. And he says, "If it doesn't bother the cattle, it won't bother me," he figures. So he moves on up closer.

And then he sees the snake coming by the next day. And he notices that the snake has a Hopi guy in his eye. But the Hopi guy is an albino. He waves at him. Waving at the things around. And he pulls on something up in the head of the snake, and the snake would yell out his sound.

And Coyote, with his curiosity, said he was going to get still closer. So he got closer the next day. And then when the snake came, he watched it, and he saw the albino Hopi in the eye of the snake. The snake didn't seem to bother anything; it just kept going on its way.

And so the next day, he got even closer. And this time, he could feel the air of the snake when it passed by. And he could hear the sounds of it. It was scary, but he wanted to test his bravery. So he got as close as he could without having the snake gobble him up, he thought. He could feel the earth shake under him. He could feel the shaking of the earth when the snake went by. But it didn't seem to bother anything. So he finally got his courage way up, and he said, "By golly, I'm gonna get right up to that snake. And I'm gonna lay right next to where he goes. And when I get back, I can tell these stories. And with my bravery, I can get all the coyote girls," he says to himself.

The next day, he gets right up to where the snake goes, and he finds out that the snake goes on a path, something shiny and hard. And it never gets off this path, or this little trail that he has. So he lays right next to the snake's trail. And then, here comes the snake, huffing and a-puffing, and a-rumbling along.

But the coyote, he wanted to test his bravery. He lay right next to it. He could feel the breeze go right by him. He was lying parallel to the snake trail. His head was flat, and his ears were flat. His tail was stretched out behind him, and the snake went by and didn't bother him. He says, "Hey, man, I can do it!" So he turns around, and gets on the other side of the trail. And then another big black snake comes along. And Coyote lies down, ears flat. He lies as flat as he could. And his tail was stretched out behind him. Here comes a big black snake rumbling by, snapping away, "Snappity-snap-snap, snappity-snap-snap." And the coyote gets overconfident. "Aw, this thing can't hurt me," he says. And so he starts to wag his tail, to show his courage. As he does, his tail gets caught under one of the snake's rollers, and it cuts off his tail. Coyote yelps. And he takes off, and he runs and runs. And he gets up to the "Homolovi," and goes to the brush and drags his butt through the sand.

And he finally finds out that his tail is missing. He finally finds out. So he runs to the water there, the Little Colorado, sticks in his little stub of a tail and cools it off. While he's doing this, he starts to think, "That thing bit my tail off. But I wonder what it did with it?" he thought. He says, "I wonder? I wonder where it went? I wonder if it's still around over there?"

So he gets up enough courage, and he says, "I'm gonna go back and see if I can find my tail." So he goes back to the spot where he was lying, and he starts sniffing along. He could see some of the blood and see some of the hair that came off. His search was so intense that he forgot about where he was. He forgot about everything around him. The world was passing by, and he was just intent on finding his tail. He didn't even know that another big black snake was coming along. And while he was still sniffing, with his head over the path of this snake, the snake rolled over him and cut his head off.

That's the story.

But the moral of the story is: Never lose your head over a piece of tail.

A Witchcraft Story

He started running until he spotted that white feather plume on top of her head.

This is a story from Walpi that I heard when I was a younger boy, and it's a story about witchcraft.

There was a couple that was newly married, and they were living alone, and they were an ideal couple, both good-looking. As time went by, the man started noticing little things that he had missed before. Like he'd never get fresh piki that was made. He'd get the piki that was made several days before, or that was given to him at a kachina dance or something. But he'd never get his fresh piki. And when he came home from the fields, he knew that fresh piki had been made because he could smell it. There's a definite smell to fresh piki.

When it's made, it's all through the house, the smell of it.

And he decided one night that he would stay awake because he had woken before nights and found her—his wife—missing from his side, on the sheepskin pelts. He thought she had gone to the bathroom, or, you know, gone to drink water or something. He hadn't paid much attention to it.

When he worked in the fields. . . .When you're up, in the Hopi Way, you stay out from sunrise to sunset, and when you get back, you're ready to sleep the night through. Get your few hours rest. Be ready for the next day. And he'd sleep like that. At night, he'd really be "out."

This one time he had it planned that he would go to the field, and instead of working—hoeing the weeds, whatever he had to do—he'd go to a wash where there were cottonwood trees and spend the afternoon there, and rest.

And so he did that. He took a nap.

When he got home, he pretended fatigue. Just a walk from the cornfield back to the village at the top of the Mesa, Walpi, would tire anybody out. But he wasn't tired. He was just waiting and watching. Looked just the same as always. And when he sat down to eat, he noticed he wasn't getting his fresh piki again.

So that was the night he was going to stay awake and see where she does go nights, because he had been noticing little mishaps, like I said before. But in the mornings when he awakened, she'd either be there beside him or up already, cooking and getting ready for the morning.

About midnight, the wife got up, and he just lay there and rolled over and pretended to snore. She got up, moved away from him, fixed up the blankets, uh, I mean coverings. They weren't blankets. There weren't woven blankets in those days. Sheepskin or pelts. She came back in a little while and pinched him on the cheek first. He just slapped at his cheek like there was a fly on his cheek. Then she pulled on his ear, and he didn't bother to check that one; he just kept on snoring.

So she left him. She started to go. When she did, he rolled over and pretended that he was still sleeping. But he kept his eye open, and he saw her go into the back storage room where the corn, beans, and chilies were kept in pottery storage jars. But he didn't move yet; he just said to himself, "I'll give her time. Maybe she'll come back out."

But she didn't come out. After a while, he went into the back room. He didn't see her, and he knew something was up, but he didn't know what. His first thoughts were that she had another lover. And so he said to himself, "Well, I'll pretend I didn't see anything." He would question her, bring it up gradually tomorrow.

So he didn't do anything that night, and he let it go through other nights. As before, he went through the same little routine of sleeping and taking a nap in the afternoon.

Then it was night. He noticed that it was certain nights that this happened, this occurrence. Just at certain times it would take place. He couldn't tell what nights it happened, but he could count the days when the next one would be. So he counted up ahead. Then he got himself ready. Took his nap.

And that night she went through the same thing. Got up. Moved away from him. I guess that was to give him the feeling of, you know, not missing her body next to him. And if she moves away a little bit and if he awakes, she can go back. He didn't wake. So then she went over and pinched him again. And pulled on his ear. Nothing happened, so she got up and went to the back room again, the storage room.

In the old days, we didn't have doors. There was just an opening. The only one that had a close-thing was the front door. Not a woven blanket.

He could see her, so he kept his eye on her this time where he could watch what was going on. So he saw her go to the back of that room where there were some big pottery storage jars. He saw her pick one up and move it aside. And then she disappeared. And he couldn't figure what happened in there. So he got up then before it got too much more complicated or she got too far away from him. He got up and went over to the back room. And he looked, and there was a little tunnel there. There was room enough for a human being to go through. But the pottery puzzled him because it was filled with beans. And when he stuck his hand in to check it, he found that there was a sifter basket hooded up underneath. Right underneath, just on the top portion of the pottery jar. Beans were scattered on top.

He couldn't figure out what was going on, but he noticed that the piki was gone, the fresh piki that had been there. And he had noticed that before he went to bed; it was in the back room. He knew where it was supposed to be. That is the first thing he missed.

Then he went through the tunnel himself. He couldn't adjust to the darkness. Like sometimes you go into a dark room, and your eyes will become adjusted. But he couldn't adjust to it, so he went by feel. Just by feel. It took him quite a while, but he finally came out on the north side of the mesa. There's an opening; you can see it. So he started going faster. And he came out there.

When he got there, there was a stairway down, like a little set of steps to get farther down. It eventually gets to the main trail off the mesa. So he knew that she wouldn't go back up the mesa.

The trail was, you know, going down, but it was also going north. And he checked the ground, and he found her track, so he knew she'd been on that trail. And he started running. He started running until he spotted that white feather plume on top of her head. And so he stopped at first and watched her. She glanced back every so often, but he followed her.

He just kept on the trail, you know; he knew about when to turn. So he kept out of sight. Behind the rocks. The brush. Whatever cover there was. And they kept going until they got up on the other side of the Gap. The other side of the mesa, the

Gap. It's called the "Wala." Up on top of that. About halfway between there and Sheep Springs.

Halfway between the Gap and Sheep Springs, there's a trail heading up. And she started going up that trail. So he just kept the same thing up: hide and seek, you know.

They got on top. He got up and looked back. He was well hidden. He kept himself well hidden. Because everybody is a warrior, he knows how to keep still without any motion. He didn't have to move. He was in a frozen state. She didn't see him, and so she went up the mesa. Got back up on the mesa where nobody lived, and he followed her.

He could tell by the feather where she was. Up on top there weren't too many brush or rocks until he got a little farther on, and he got into cedar trees. So then he got closer. He got closer and closer, going from tree to tree behind her.

She got to a certain spot up there on top of that mesa, and she looked around. She kept looking and looking and looking. He kind of felt that she felt his presence, but he wasn't sure. He just kept still, and he tried to keep his thought going the other way. Thinking about rabbit hunting or the cornfield, or this and that. He knew that if his thoughts were on her she would feel it. So he used his thoughts also. To think about other things. He turned away for a few seconds every time she, you know, looked up.

He saw her open the ground. Or she tapped on the ground, is what it was. She tapped on the ground and it opened. Then a man came out, and she went in. And he stood watch. Kept watching. Looking, looking, looking. And after she was gone quite a while, then he went over. And this time he was watching carefully.

He said he would give them time, "So that they won't suspect that I'm following." These were his thoughts.

So he waited around up there for quite a while. And then he heard singing. And it wasn't just two voices; it was more. He couldn't figure out what it was.

And when his curiosity couldn't keep up, he went over closer to the opening. And there was a ground-covering. It was just a disguised cover on the ground, and he could see the one section of it. I think it was a sifter-type thing. You know, woven, like a reed covering, but it had plants and things on top to give it a camouflage, but he could see inside, through cracks and openings. And he could see his wife inside. And he could see some other people he recognized. And he could see some others that he didn't recognize at all. They were all in there.

It was just like a normal kiva gathering, where they go in and talk and greet each other and shake hands and this and that. Everything looked just like a normal kiva gathering. But it wasn't a normal kiva.

And he kept his watch there, his vigil. Toward midnight at a certain time, they all got ready for something that was going to happen. He didn't know what; he was just watching.

And then it occurred to him that it was a full moon that

night. He started thinking back, "It's been every full moon that she has been doing this." He just counted days before, but now he knew.

He kept looking in, and then he saw them getting ready. They were putting on skins. Pelts, I guess you would call them. Feathers and things like this. It looked like they were getting ready for a dance. In a dance, they use woven stuff; these were skins. He was still puzzled.

And then they got together and made an altar, and they were doing their chants. When they got to a certain point in it, they would jump through a yucca hoop. And when the first guy jumped through, the leader—I think he was supposed to be a deer—he jumped through, but he hadn't turned into a full animal deer. He was half animal and half man. So when he came back through, he said something's wrong.

So they tried another person. They said, "Maybe it's you. Did you expose us to someone?"

So they tried another person. The same thing happened. He turned half wolf and half man. So then they knew what it was as soon as that second occurrence happened.

Then the ones with the pelts of the fast animals, like the bear and the wolf, the puma, deer, they went out. As soon as they got out, they caught him. It was his watching that caused the incompletion. They could not complete their ritual, so they caught him and brought him in and tried to decide what to do, because death was the penalty.

He saw his wife there, but she wouldn't take pity on him or anything. And so they gave him a choice: he could join them and they would let him live.

He asked them what they were going to do, and they told him, "You'll find out. But you have to agree first. Either that or death."

So he chose to go along with them, with their witchcraft rituals.

So they went through the initiation acts, things they normally go through. The feather ceremonies. Washing of the hair. The cornmeal, and things like this. They got him ready. But there were no more pelts left. There was only one, and that was the turkey. So he wound up with the turkey pelt, with the turkey feathers still on it.

And they went through their jumping-through ceremony. Each time they jumped through the hoop, they would turn into the animal of the pelt they had on. When his turn came, he tried it, and he *did.* He turned into a turkey. But he wasn't used to flying. It was his legs that were strong.

And when they all got through, they left the kiva. They were going to a meeting where all the witches meet. Some place in Lukachukai. That's where all the witches from all over the country, I guess, meet. Even from Mexico. They were having their big meeting and feast there that night. That's why they just gave him a quick initiation.

And so they started out. The others were the animals with

strength. They knew the route; they knew where to go, so they just took off. And him being a turkey, he couldn't use his wings that well. He tired out right away. His wife kept coming back after him and told him not to give up: "We've got to make that place over there."

And he kept trying and trying, but he couldn't do it. He finally told her, "Go ahead. You go ahead, and I'll catch up later."

The other animals went on ahead. He tried to catch up, but he couldn't. And he gave up. He quit and sat down. Then when that happened, he turned into a turkey permanently. Never could come back out of it.

So that's one of the punishments for trying to get into something you don't belong to. Getting involved in something you know nothing about.

Poowak Wuhti

This is my story. There lived a long time ago in the village of Keuchaptuvela, a village below the present site of Walpi—where the people lived before they moved up to the present site—a man who was a good farmer. He had a lot of plants, and he grew good crops. When he gathered in his crops, he had plenty. He would always go to the fields to check his plants, and when he came home in the evenings, his wife would always meet him and help bring in the corn. "I have lots and lots of corn. I'm going to make several piles in the field tomorrow, and I'm going to husk it," he told his wife.

"That's good," his wife said. "Tomorrow maybe I'll make

"You're taking too much time, Whoo, oo-oo," it said.

us a bundle of food and go with you."

Coming home from the fields each day, the man would hunt and kill cottontail rabbits, and his wife would skin them and roast them. But he would never get any rabbit stew; they would only eat the insides of the rabbit, something called *kwitaviki.*

One morning, he went in the back room of his house, and he saw jackrabbits and cottontails hanging from a beam. They were dried, roasted and dried. "So this is what she's doing. That's why we never had any rabbit stew. I keep hunting and hunting, but I never eat any rabbit stew." This is what he was thinking. "Maybe today she's going to make piki. I see her pot with the batter." As he looked around, he saw a fireplace. There was a pot in it, and there was a fire under it. The man looked at it, and walked over and looked inside. She had broken the rabbit carcasses in half and boiled them like that. "Oh, this evening we're going to have rabbit. Looks like we're really going to have a feast tonight."

So he went to the field to husk corn. When he looked in the back room the next time, he saw piki, a whole row of rolled piki. He was really happy when he got home at noon. This is when he saw the piki and the stew.

When he got home in the evening, it was suppertime. The food was placed on the floor. There was dusty food and a blue corn gruel. This is what was laid on the floor. "I wonder what happened to the stew? Why are we eating these things," the man was thinking, but he didn't say anything to his wife. He remembered seeing the fresh piki, but it wasn't on the floor with the other food. "I wonder what she did with it that we're not eating it," he thought. So he ate and moved away. He kept thinking about it, though, but he didn't say anything to his wife. "I'm really sleepy," he said. "I'll pretend to sleep and see what she does." This is what he thought. He knew he had seen the stew and the piki, and they hadn't eaten any of it. He wondered. So he sat down and smoked his pipe next to the fireplace.

It was late in the evening. "Yes, I'm tired," the man said. "I made several piles of corn in the field today."

"Is that right," the wife said. "Tomorrow we'll go together. I'll husk while you carry them home," she told her husband.

"That's good; we'll do it that way," he said, but he was still thinking.

He was pretending sleepiness like he just couldn't keep awake. His wife said. "Shall we go to bed? You must be tired," his wife said to him.

"Okay, we might as well go to bed," her husband said. So they made their bedding, and he lay down. His wife lay down with him. Pretty soon the man began snoring as if he were asleep. A little later, the woman got up. She went to her husband. He looked like he was asleep; he had his arms over his head. He had hair in his armpits, so she pulled a hair. He didn't move. "I knew this woman was up to something," he thought to himself, but he pretended to sleep and snored louder. "I'll see what she's up to."

She lay down with him again. In a little while, she got up again. She pulled a hair from his (pointing to the genitals). He still didn't move. She tried it from his back, and he still didn't move. So she lay down again. Then she put her face right over his face and looked at his nose. There was hair in his nose, so she pulled a hair out of one side. He still didn't move. So she got up. "He must really be asleep," she said. Her husband was pretending to be asleep, snoring away.

He heard a noise outside. It was an owl. "Whoo, whoo, oo-oo," it said. "You're taking too much time. Whoo, oo-oo," it said.

"Because he didn't go to sleep right away," she whispered back.

So they were supposed to go to a witch house. She started to get ready to go. Later on the owl came back. The man was still pretending to be sleeping, but he knew everything that was going on. Then his wife went into the back room. And she was brushing her hair in there. She put on her *manta*. Then she got her bundle. She got something out of another bundle and laid it next to the man. She said, "Keep him sleeping. Keep him sleeping tight."

The owl was making noise outside again, and he told her: "You're taking too much time."

"Just wait for me," she whispered back to the owl. Then she

picked up her pottery full of rabbit stew, and she picked up her bundle of rolled piki. She handed it to the owl outside. Then she went out, following him carrying her bundle of piki.

As soon as they got out, the man got up and went to see what was going on. There was a skeleton lying next to him. He was angry, so he picked up the skeleton and threw it against the wall. He said, "Why are you putting this next to me," he said as if to his wife. He looked outside, and he could see that there was bright moonlight. He could see them walking toward the east. They were going out toward the mud flats.

A witch house can be just anyplace. That's where they were going, to a witch house. The owl was taking the woman there. There was a little spring in the area, and it was close to that.

The man began to follow them. He was sneaking behind them. When they got to the place, they went inside the kiva. It was just a flat place, and straw rafters were on top of the kiva, so he peeped in through the top. He saw there were a lot of people in there.

"You're sure late. You took too much time," the witch people said.

"My husband didn't go to sleep right away," she answered.

He listened from the top; he could see them clearly from there. There were a lot of them. There were a lot of women in there too, all sitting together.

"Okay, let's not waste any more time and go," the head man said. He went to the altar first. A lot of things were made into the altar. A man turned a somersault over the altar, and he didn't turn into anything. When he got up, he was still a Hopi.

"Something's happened," he said. "Someone is watching from some place." They went up to the top to look, but they didn't find anybody, so they went back into the kiva. The husband was still watching from the top, hidden by the covering which was made of reeds. This time a girl went over the altar. She turned a somersault and came out. She didn't turn into anything either. She was still a Hopi when she got up.

"Something is wrong. I wonder what it is," they said.

"I really think somebody's watching," she said. Then they got out and started looking again. Again they didn't find him. The man who had brought his wife, the owl-man, he was her witch-husband, and he went out and looked carefully. He kept searching, and he found the man under the covering of reeds.

"You better come in," he told him. "Come into the kiva," he said. So he went in.

The man's wife saw him, recognized him, and called him. "Come here," she said.

They told him, "You have to join us now. We're going to a witch-gathering to have a feast tomorrow night, so we have to turn into animals by going over the altar. You will have to go out and get a niece, nephew, or your younger brother and kill him with witchcraft magic. You have to get their heart. It has to be someone that you really love that you get the heart out of," they told him.

So he went home, and while he was looking over his nieces and nephews, he felt sorry for them. He couldn't choose any of them or kill any of them. Then he thought of his pet turkey. He said, "I'll go to my turkey," he said, "I love my turkey." So he went after his turkey, killed it, and took out its heart.

The next night, he went back to the witch kiva. He took the heart of the turkey over to the witch altar. When his turn came, he rolled a somersault over the altar and turned into a turkey. When they started to go, his wife had trouble getting him to keep up with the others. Turkeys can't move fast. They were going to a witch-gathering to a big feast.

There were a lot of people there at the gathering already when the man and his wife got there. When they got there, there were head-washing bowls, four of them in a row, and the people were washing their hair in the bowl of their choice.

Some of them were really evil. "The ones that swallowed snakes," is the term for them, the really evil ones.

They washed their hair in the first bowl. And there was a second bowl. This one was for those who didn't want to be that evil; they wanted to learn witchcraft just so they could grow good crops and grow good plants. And there was a third bowl. They wash their hair to become good thieves, to gain material wealth. And some want to become good farmers, but they want to use witchcraft to grow good crops. They wash their hair in another bowl. Each chooses what kind of witch power they want.

Then they ate. They ate well. The husband, the turkey-man, went to sleep. When he woke up, there was nothing left at all. He was on a little pinnacle of a cliff. He couldn't turn over or even move much. "Gollee, how am I going to get home from here? I had no business coming here," he said. He was still lying there, and he heard something coming. It sounded like laughter: "Ha-ha, ha-ha." Something was making that noise. It got closer to him. They were the Bluebird Girls. They brought some "ko̲-mi," corn cakes and piñon nuts. They brought him water in piñon shells. These Bluebird Girls, they fed him that first day. And then the Bluebird Girls went on their way.

The next day, he heard something else again. When he looked down, there were Chipmunks that had come to help him this time. They brought the same things that the Girls had brought: "ko̲-mi," or corn cakes, piñons, and water in piñon shells. One of the Chipmunks said to him: "Tomorrow we'll bring you regular food," he said.

He couldn't turn or even move. If he did, he would fall off of the pinnacle. He listened and heard something. It was a Navajo Kachina Uncle making a noise. This is what he hears: "Ooooo." That's what the sound was. It was the Navajo Kachina Uncle saying to him, "Tomorrow morning the witches from the village of Walpi will come to you."

The next evening his wife was acting as a *Hahay'e Wuhti* kachina. But earlier, the Spider Woman came to the man, and she sat on his shoulder, instructing him. "They're going to come and try to break you. They're going to ask you to go down with them, but don't do it. Don't go with them. Here is some strong medicine. Chew it and spit it all over them. The ones who are going to come are witches. They're going to come with a water snake or water serpent. The witch-people are going to be inside that snake, and they will make it appear alive. They will be turned into a huge water snake. They are going to ask you to come down, but don't agree to go with them. Chew this medicine and spit it on them, and they will crumble. They'll die." His wife really was the *Hahay'e.*

The water serpent told him, "Grab onto my horn, and I'll get you down." He asked the same question four times, but the man wouldn't do it. Then he chewed the medicine and sprayed the serpent with it. The serpent crashed to the ground. And when it crashed, the man saw that it was full of witches, witch-people that were in that snake. When they fell, they cried because several of them were hurt and dying.

Then the Navajo Kachina Uncle brought him some food. He said, "Tomorrow I'll get you down. And this time you must come with me," he said. The next morning, he woke up, and something was making a noise at the bottom of the cliff. He looked down and saw that it was the Chipmunks. One of the Chipmunks was planting something there; by using his powers, he made two trees grow. When it was time for the sheep to come home, the Chipmunk had made them grow up to the point where the man was level with the trees. They were Douglas firs. So he caught hold of a branch of one of the Douglas fir trees and gripped it. Then he started going down, holding on to each one, one hand on each tree. Shimmying, ladder-style, he went down. Then he got down to the bottom, and Spider Woman gave him instructions, "Don't go home to your wife. Tell a lie; tell the people that you've been hunting and that you've been to a hunter's camp. Here is some medicine. Your wife will come over and make *pikami* for you. So go to your mother's house. Don't act as if anything happened in front of her. Don't say anything cruel to her, just act nice. She'll come over and eat with you at your mother's house. She'll bring her *pikami* pudding to eat with you. When she's eating her pudding, put this medicine in her food. But do this after your people have eaten. Let them eat first, and you eat alone with her."

So he did everything he was told. When he got to his mother's house, they were eating together. When they got through, his wife ate with him. She ate the medicine, and the medicine got her. She jumped up and threw off her *manta.* She threw all her other clothes off. She was going; she would run and make hard copulation movements against the wall. She went crazy. Then she started running, and nobody tried to stop her. They were afraid and just watched her. She got to a high cliff, and she jumped off the cliff. She threw herself over the cliff and ended her life.

This is how he returned her mistreatment.

This is the end of the story.

Hano Wuhti

"Hano Wuhti" ("Hano Lady") was narrated by a Hopi who is descended from the Hano People.

An explanation of a few specific references may be helpful. In references to the sorcerers, the word "Quitam" was used by the storyteller in the original Hopi version. "Quita" is the word used for feces, and "quitam" are those people like feces. The drill that the witch-bird uses to remove the woman's heart is of the old type, made of a stick, a wooden disc at the base, and two buckskin thongs attached to a crosspiece. The drill primarily was used for making holes in turquoise and shell.

She kept right on grinding at her grinding stone.

A long time ago at the east end of First Mesa, in the village of Hano, there lived a woman. She was a good woman. Pretty. And a modest woman. She hardly ever went to watch the dances, but instead, stayed inside her house working. Everyone liked her very much. She had a good husband. He was a good worker. A hard worker, spending most of his time in the fields.

The woman, however, was unfaithful behind her husband's back. When he would go out at night to the kiva or on business, her lover would come to pay her a visit. He was a Laguna man. He brought her belts, moccasins, buckskins, beads, concho belts, and *mantas.* He gave gifts to her for her sexual favors. She couldn't wear these things, of course; she just hid them away.

This is the way the woman was secretly living. She lived with her father and mother, her younger brother, and an older brother.

In the village of Hano at one time, the houses were stacked on top of each other, and she lived on top, in one of these houses.

The members of the Plaza Kiva were sorcerers, and these men were desirous of this woman. They wanted to get her for one of their own members. But she never would come out. The members of the Plaza Kiva wanted to get her out in the open so that they could get a good look at her, but she very modestly stayed inside her house.

So they made a plan with the Southside Kiva, the one near

the road in Hano. To gain her attention, they tried various tricks. They kept looking up at her house while they were performing their dances, but she wouldn't come out. "I wonder how we can get her to come out," were their constant thoughts. These were wishful thoughts, coveting thoughts.

Now as I said, the woman couldn't wear the gifts that her lover from Laguna gave her. She hid them in her back storage room.

Now her younger brother was a member of the Plaza Kiva, but he was not a sorcerer; he didn't know the "two ways," the sorcerer's road. Whenever he was in the kiva, he would only sit back and watch the others in the lower level of the kiva. He knew that they were making plans, and that they were consorting with the Southside Kiva. He knew they were planning to play tricks on some pretty woman, to get her to come out of her house.

So the kachinas, the Mudheads and the Racing Kachinas, went ahead and got ready for their dance. But still she wouldn't come out. She kept right on grinding at her grinding stone. She sang as she ground, always thinking about Hopi foods and their preparation. While the other people were outside having fun, she sang and continued to grind. Even when night fell, she would still be grinding.

This made the members of the Plaza Kiva angry, for they couldn't get her to come out. They couldn't break her. They wanted to get her for the wife of one of their members so badly that they would try all kinds of different things. "I wonder what we can do to get her to come out?" was the constant talk of the sorcerers in the kiva.

Finally, they decided if they couldn't have her, no one else would. Now there was one really good sorcerer, an artist in witchcrafts. So the other members approached him. And he agreed to fix things so that the young woman would come out. She was a young woman, a good woman, a beautiful woman.

After four days, the sorcerers made a "ti puch qua," a bird that looks like a rock wren. They instructed the bird to go to the woman's house and fly to her window. He was to sit on the window and show himself to her. Maybe she would like him. "If she says anything to you, don't fly away. Try to get closer to her. She will throw you her corn crumbs. Pick them up and eat them." This is what they told the bird to do.

As so he did. He flew out of the kiva, and went straight to her and sat on her window. The lady was grinding and singing. She raised her head and saw the bird at the window. "Pretty thing, you pretty little bird." She said this. "You're really a pretty bird. How can I make you my pet? Thank you for coming to me, you pretty thing." Then the bird flew down to her, right down on top of the box holding her grinding stone. She threw crumbs to him, and the bird began to eat. She threw more and more crumbs to him. He ate them before he flew back to the kiva.

The sorcerers had instructed the bird not to let her catch

him yet. She tried to catch him in her blanket. "How can I catch you and make you my pet?" she said to herself. Then she resumed her grinding. The little bird stayed a little longer and then finally flew away, back to the kiva.

That was the bird's first visit to her. When he got back to the kiva, the sorcerers said, "Owi, yes. How did you find things?" they asked.

"I found things just as you predicted they would be. She said, 'You're sure a pretty bird. How can I catch you so I can make you my pet?' this is what she said," the bird reported.

"Okay, you will go again. This time you can sit on top of her corn-grinding box. When she spits, you pick up the spittle with your beak."

"Okay," the bird said, "I'll not waste any time."

The next day he flew up again to the same window. "Gee, you're sure a pretty bird," she said again. He flew down to the corn-grinding box. Whenever she would spit, he would go and pick up her spittle. He was a witch-bird, so he could pick it all up. She tried to grab the bird, but he flew away.

This is what he did. And he flew back to the kiva and told them what had happened. They asked him, "What did you find out? What did you hear?"

He said, "Everything was just as you predicted. She said, 'You're such a pretty bird. I would like to catch you for a pet.' That is what she said." And he spit up the spittle that he had picked up from her. And it turned into water.

"That's good. Thank you," the sorcerers said. "You have to go again. This time you have to go and just fly around, and then climb up on her back. When you get on her back, just sit there and gain her confidence." They gave him a wooden drill. They said, "With this drill, you are to take out her heart."

So he flew out of the kiva again and back to her same little window. "Come in," she said.

He was hopping around on her corn-grinding box. Then he got on top of her hand. She didn't bother him when he got on her hand, so he climbed up her arm and got on the back of her neck. She kept singing away. Grinding corn. Then he got on her back, right at the spot where her heart was. He took out his wooden drill and twisted it quickly. He pulled out her heart by using witchcraft. Then he took her heart back to the kiva. The sorcerers and the witchcraft men were very happy. "Thank you, thank you," they said. "Tomorrow morning we will do some work to get ready for the dancing and gambling."

They took the things from him, for tomorrow they were going to have a dart-throwing contest with the Southside Kiva. They were going to make a hoop with the heart of the young woman in the center of the hoop.

So they are going to gamble with the Southside Kiva, the "Road Kiva." The woman's husband didn't know about this, even though he was a member of the Southside Kiva. So that night, the woman slept, and she didn't know that her heart was missing.

The next day toward evening, the gamblers came out, both kivas, one against the other. The Plaza Kiva called the Southside Kiva to gamble with them. At about the time when the sheep were coming home, time to bring them in, that's when the gamblers came out. They had prizes of sweet corn and corn cakes. They took their prizes to the plaza. The kachinas came, lots of them, and many people gathered around. A crowd soon grew. The woman's younger brother was with the group from the Plaza Kiva, the sorcerers, and her husband from the Southside Kiva also was taking part. Her mother and father were dressed, and they went to watch. They had a little platform on their house, up on top, and they watched from there.

The lady with no heart got curious and wanted to see what was going on below, so she put on her best clothes and brushed her hair which was long and reached down to her ankles, and went out to watch. She brushed her hair, got up, and went down, and stood in the doorway. While she was standing in the doorway a Mudhead threw his dart, hitting the center of the hoop where her heart was. She was just taking a step through the doorway when she fell. The crowd got excited and ran to see what had happened to her. Before the people reached her, she was dead. She had died instantly. The younger brother saw the crowd near his house. The Mudheads and the kachinas were still playing their games, and they didn't know what had happened yet. When the younger brother saw the crowd of people gathered at his house, he ran to see what had happened. "I'd better go see what it is," he said. He was still dressed as "Kuyemsi," but he ran anyway. When he got there, he saw his sister lying in the doorway. Then he remembered that he was still dressed as a "Kuyemsi," so he ran back to the kiva, undressed, took off his mudhead, and put on his everyday clothes. Then he hurried back to his sister. He began to cry, "My poor older sister; what has happened to you? There doesn't seem to be anything wrong with you. This is all so sudden." His mother and father were crying very hard.

A little later, her husband came. "What's happening?" he asked.

"We don't know. She was going to see the dance and she just crumbled at the doorway. She's dead already."

They tried to revive her, but they couldn't. So they decided to bury her right away. In the old days, burial was quick, the same day. So the young woman's father did the Burial Way for her. "Poor thing, my daughter. There was nothing wrong, and you died," he was crying.

So late in the evening, must have been about dusk, they took her down for burial. They went down through the Gap going toward the South, along the horse trail, to a yellow-faced rock butte at the bottom of the mesa. To the west of that, they made a burial grave in the sand. Only the men went, just the fathers. In the old days, that's how it was. So they made a grave, a round, circular grave, about four feet around and five feet deep. They placed her upright in it. Then they made beams going across the top opening and they cross-beamed it. Then they plastered it with clay, and covered it on top with sand. They buried her properly.

Now it was late at night, so they left her and went home.

Her husband just couldn't believe that she was gone. She had been healthy. She wasn't sickly. Nothing had been wrong with her. He just couldn't believe that she was gone. That night everybody cried. Toward morning, everybody except the husband had gone to sleep. He couldn't go to sleep.

Dawn came. First the light to the East, then the sun finally rose.

He had a field to work, and so he went to the field. But on the way to the field, and all day working there, his thoughts were constantly on his wife. "Why did she die?" He couldn't get over it. Late in the evening, he went home, to the girl's parents. "I wonder what happened to her?" he asked.

"We don't know," they answered. "It didn't seem as though such a thing could ever happen. But I guess things do happen this way sometimes."

Twilight came and the man left the house. While he was setting on the rooftop, he thought to himself, "I think I'll go over to the grave and see for myself. And then I'll know that she is really dead. That it's true." He got ready and went down the same trail that the fathers had taken when they took her to bury her. As he approached Yellow Rocks, he stopped.

"Maybe I shouldn't go over," he said. "Maybe she didn't truly love me. Maybe she didn't really have any feelings for me and just left me." He stopped there for a while and considered giving up. Then he changed his mind again. "I've got to go see for myself or I'll never know." So he went on toward the grave.

When he got close to the grave, about two steps short of it, he kneeled down. He could see a light in the grave, through the beams over the top. "So this is how it is," he said to himself. So he lay down on top of the grave and looked down into it. As he was looking into the grave, he saw his wife; she was brushing her hair. She was taking care of her hair. "I thought so," he said, "there's something going on. Something is wrong. She died, but she's not dead. There's some reason for sitting there," he was thinking to himself.

The woman turned her head upward. Looked up and saw her husband. "Oh, my husband," she said, "Why did you come?" she said to him. "You shouldn't be looking at me from there. You ought to go home," she told him.

"Yes, my wife. I had to come. I am hurting, and I am lonesome for you. That's why I came to see your grave. I couldn't believe that you're really dead."

"Dead people at this time, the four days before going to The Place of the Dead, are like this. We wake up and brush our hair and fix ourselves up, as you see me. This is what dead people do at this time. So now you know, and when you see other people, tell them not to brush their hair." This is what she told him.

"Okay," the man said. "I'm sorry I lost you."

"But you can't be here. I have three more days to be here and then I am going to leave you. You can't go with me," she said, "because I'm going to the Place of the Dead."

"But I think I can go with you," he said. "There must be some way. I want to go with you. I want to be with you."

"But you can't go," she said. "You're not dead," she said. "If you go with me you won't be able to see; I will be invisible. All you can see is the feather on top of my head, the breath-feather. We're going to be going south. If you really are going to go with me, remember that all you can see is my feather. You have to make moccasins. You will need plenty of moccasins to follow my feather, for we're going to The Place of the Dead. The way is steep and rocky, so if you're going to go with me, make plenty of moccasins."

"Okay," the man said. "I'll do that," he said. "I'm lonesome for you and I need you. I want to be with you and I'll go anywhere to be with you," he told her.

"Okay," she said. While they were still talking, the yellow light of morning came. Suddenly, there was no hole. No beams. The ground was as before. There was only the grave.

"So this is how it is," the man said. "I have to go home now and start making moccasins, because I want to go and I know

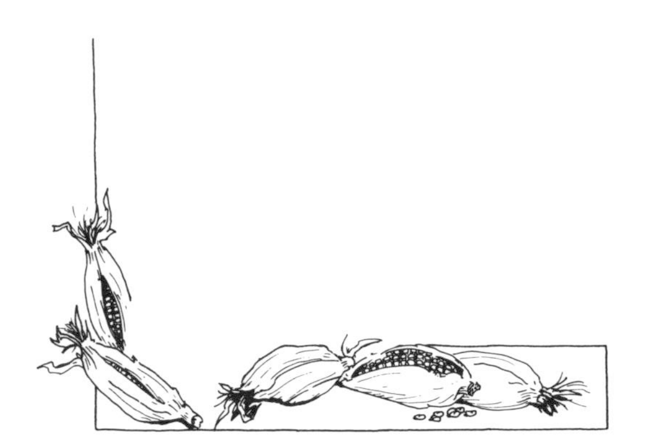

that it's rough and rocky, and a steep trail. So he left and went home.

When he got to his in-law's house, he didn't tell the mother or father where he had been that night. When he got home that morning, he got out his cowhide and his tanned deerskin. He knew how to make moccasins, and he started. He started to sew them quickly, just as fast as he could. He was pretty fast at it. Late in the afternoon, he had already finished one pair. By then, it was time to eat. He sat down with his in-laws to have supper with them. He started thinking again, "Maybe I should go to the grave again."

When it got late that night, he took off down to the grave again. This time he knew the trail and what was going on, so he hurried without any hesitation. He went straight to the grave. It didn't take long. When he saw the grave, it was lighted, just as before.

"My husband, you're here again. You shouldn't do this. I am unnatural; you shouldn't come here."

"I miss you. I had to see you again," he said. So they started talking to each other about various things, how the people are living, prophecies, and such.

"My husband," she said to him, "you shouldn't be wearing yourself out for me. You can't come with me; you're not a dead person."

"Yes, I know," he said, "but I really want to go with you. I love you."

"But my husband, there are things that have to be done yet. There are things that you don't know about. I don't want to tell you about these things. But if you insist on going, you will find out, and you will be hurt. You see, I haven't been what you thought I was. I haven't been the good wife you thought."

"Is that true?" the man asked. "It doesn't matter. I have to see for myself, so I'm going," he said.

They were still talking to each other when it got light again. As soon as the yellow light came, the hole disappeared. There was just a regular grave with normal dirt on top of it. So he went home and started making moccasins again. This was the second day. He made another pair of moccasins and night fell again.

That night, he went straight to the grave.

The girl's mother made him a bundle of food to take with him, because he had lied, saying he was going to a Navajo camp. He lied to her and told her to make him a bundle of food to take on his trip to the Navajo camp. She said, "Please don't leave us here. I know our daughter is gone, but we still depend on you," his mother-in-law told him. "Don't leave us in this poor condition that we're in."

"Okay," the man said. So he picked up his old blanket, and he got his "ate'e," a little white cape with red and black borders on two sides, and his moccasins. He rolled them up in his blanket and tied the bundle on his back, and went straight to the grave.

When he got there, there was a light in the grave. The woman was brushing her hair again. She sure was pretty. She looked up and said, "Did you come again? Are you really going with me?"

He said, "Yes. I brought my things with me. I don't have to go back to the village again. I can go with you."

"My poor husband," she said, "you can't go with me. You have nothing to do in The Place of the Dead." That was what the woman said.

"That's all right; I've made up my mind to go with you."

"Well, I told you to watch for the white feather in my hair. That's all you'll be able to see. So be careful and keep it in sight."

"Okay, I'll do that," the husband said. "I'll keep watching for the hair-feather, but I really want to go with you—wherever you go."

"Did you make enough moccasins?" she asked him.

"Yes, I made four pair."

"Did you bring something for you to eat, something to keep you alive?"

He said, "Yes."

"Okay, I see," she said. "So now we can get ready," she said.

He was sitting, looking at his wife, and he went to sleep at the edge of her grave. He woke up with a strange feeling. There was nobody in the grave, and the sun was just coming up.

There was a thunderclap-like noise, like a big breath. It was the spirit of the woman coming out of the grave. When he looked to the south, he could see the white feather—the plume. It was moving, so he jumped up and started to follow.

He was trotting behind it. And then it stopped. And he walked faster, and then started trotting again. Going, going, heading toward the South. Still going and going. He got to some white cliffs. As he was getting close to the white cliffs, up there [pointing] somewhere, it became night. He began to search for her, the white feather. He thought she might have gone into the darker cliffs, to those red cliffs [pointing]. "I'll follow her into the red cliffs." When he next spotted her, it was in a grave, just the same as the one they had buried her in. She was sitting in the same type of grave, and there was light in it, just like before. From the top of the grave, he started talking to his wife.

My husband doesn't know what is happening, but he still won't give up, and he's still going with me, she thought to herself. "You should go home," she said. "It's still a long way," she said. "From here on it's going to get rough."

They were still talking when the dawn light came. When the light came, again he couldn't see her. So he looked to the south and saw the white breath-feather, and he started to follow it again.

It was getting to be noontime now. He was getting tired, and the moccasins on his feet were getting worn out. His moccasins were all beaten up. "It's about noontime now," he thought. "This is why I made so many moccasins." So he took off his moccasins and threw them into the bushes, and put on a new pair. He started running and picked up speed. He ran, following the breath-feather until he got close to her. Then he trotted, and slowed down some until he was just walking fast.

That's how he was walking when he got to the cliffs. It was like an oven and this is where he ran into cactus. Wherever he stepped, he would step into some type of cactus. Then he came to some red cliffs again. He was just getting to the bottom of these cliffs when he had to start uphill. He was almost to the top of the cliffs and it became night again. And he rested and slept for a while.

He woke up and went to the grave. He could see his wife and talk to her again. She said, "Why are you still following me and tormenting yourself? There are different things that you are going to witness that you might not like. But you seem to have made up your mind, and you're still going. There must be a very strong reason for you to continue with me this far. We're getting very close to The Place of the Dead, so watch carefully and observe everything that happens. From here on, it's going to get *really* rough. It's going to be steep and the ground is rough. You'll wear out another pair of moccasins tomorrow."

"Is that right?" the man said. "I still have some moccasins left."

"You still have things to eat?" she asked.

"Yes, I still have a little bit left," he said, "but I think I have enough. I think I have enough to get there."

"I see," the woman said. "Now say a little prayer and get some rest."

He slept and rested for a little while. Morning came. He looked to the south again and he remembered that he had some place to go. He could hardly see the feather. He stood up and put his hand over his eyes to "sight in," and finally he saw the feather. It was a little speck, and it was way ahead of him. So he took off. He was a good runner, so he started running. He ran faster, then as fast as he could. Before long, he caught up with the feather again. So he slowed down and walked fast, as before. He was getting to a place far to the South. There was nothing but cactus and thorns. He checked his moccasins, and they were getting worn out. He was now walking on rough rocks—lava rocks—and he tripped a lot of times, almost falling. Going on like this, he finally came out onto a chasm, right in the middle of nowhere. He stopped and sat down. He took off his moccasins and started pulling thorns out of them, checking his feet. He threw these moccasins away. They were worn out in one morning. "That's another pair of moccasins," he thought. He says to himself, "I wonder if I made enough?" This is what he was thinking. Now he started to get worried. "I wonder if I made enough? She told me not to come. That's okay, I made up my own mind. I want to see what happens.

Maybe tomorrow we'll get to the place." The man was thinking and talking to himself.

Then he started running again to catch up with the woman. He got to rocks with sharp edges, and was having a hard time running. He couldn't run well. From here on, it got dark. Thick trees. He could barely see her; just once in a while he could spot the feather. He continued on, following the feather. Then the feather went out of sight. He came to a place where there was a deep canyon. He looked down. There was a steep drop, but he could see the white feather down in the canyon. He kept looking down. "How am I going to get down there?" he said. "I wonder how I'll catch up with the feather now?" he said. While he was still watching, something came up behind him. Something came up with a little plaque, slipped it under his feet, and he began to fly. The plaque took him down into the canyon. He landed on the canyon, got off, and started walking again.

He heard somebody talking to him. It was the breath-feather that was talking. "My husband," she said, "you listen carefully now. You listen very carefully, and hear what I have to say."

"Okay," the man said.

"To the south of here there's a big open space. There's water. It's a lake. Can you see it? That's where we're going to," she said. "There's a closure up there, a dam-like. That's where we're going," she said.

"Okay," the man said. And from there on, the woman talked through the feather.

"Listen and watch. We're getting close now," she said. "You still have moccasins?" she asked.

"I threw one pair to the north of here, and I still have one pair left. Those are the ones I have on now."

"Okay, we're getting close," she said. "We're almost finished," she said.

"Okay," the man said.

"We're getting closer now. There's the big lake."

He kept looking and watching. They came to an opening, a meadow-like. In it were a lot of animals, horses, burros, mules. There were all kinds of animals. There wasn't any kind of animal that wasn't in there.

They were getting closer now. Then the wife told the man, "My husband," she said, "listen carefully now."

"Okay," the man said, "I will listen."

Getting closer . . . getting closer. Just about a mile, they could see. Then the wife started taking quick breaths. She began to cry. Then she began to sing at this point:

My husband! My husband! My husband!
My poor husband. Listen my husband.
I have been untrue.
I have been with Mule Man.
This is what happened.

This is what happened.
This is what happened in my former life.

And then with a sharp intake of breath, she cried again.

They were getting closer. They got to the lake now. Just four more steps to get into the water. To the south there was a mule. The big black mule started crying. He cried and cried. Then he reared and started running, running toward them. The woman just kept going to get to the edge of the water. The big black mule kept running, running toward them. Then the mule jumped on the woman and began having intercourse with her. She let him and he kept on having intercourse with her. The mule took her into the water, to the middle of the lake. They both went in and sank into the water.

"So this is it. So this is what happened in her former life," he said. "And I thought there was nothing wrong with her. I thought she was a good woman. She was doing this behind my back." The man felt sorry for himself. "Now I've seen it with my own eyes, so I have to believe."

So the man turned around and headed for home. He started to trot. He got so far and then he looked back. Something was after him—something with a big bush head. And ugly. Something frightening. And then the man took off and started running as fast as he could.

The woman who was running after him was a ghost-woman. She had turned into a ghost-woman now.

He got a little further, and he heard somebody working. The man ran on and stopped. It was a gopher. Gopher was working in his field. "My Grandfather," the man said, "there is a ghost-lady chasing me! Please hide me," he says.

"I have no place for you to hide," he said.

"Quick, hide me, my Grandfather," he said.

"I don't know where to hide you," the gopher said. He had a pouch in his cheek. He said, "I'll use magic. Make you small and put you inside my cheek."

Pretty soon, the ghost-lady came. "Aye," she said. "I've been looking for my husband. Have you seen him?"

"No," the gopher said.

"This is the place where his tracks end," she thought to herself. They don't go anywhere from here. He's got to be here." She used her witchcraft to see him. And she spotted him. She slapped Gopher's cheek, and her husband popped out and started running again.

And then the ghost-lady started chasing him. He ran and ran until he met a *Heheah.* He was weeding, hoeing his field. That's who he came to this time. "Grandfather," he said, "Grandfather, please hide me; there's a ghost-lady chasing me."

"I don't know where to hide you," *Heheah* said.

"Just hide me anywhere. Please, my Grandfather."

Heheah cut a big pile of weeds. He lifted the weeds and told the man to get underneath. When he did, *Heheah* covered him up with the tumbleweeds and all kinds of weeds that he had chopped.

Pretty soon the ghost-lady caught up with him. She said, "Aye. I'm looking for my husband. Did anybody come here?" she asked.

Heheah said, "Nobody's been here. I haven't seen anybody."

She said, "These footprints come this far, and they don't go anywhere."

"Well, look for yourself," he said. And she went to the pile of weeds. The man jumped up and started running again. The woman started following him, running. They ran for a long distance. The man was running back toward home, through what is now the White Cone area.

He ran through what is now a Navajo settlement. There he ran into a frog. He got to the frog and said, "Grandfather, can you hide me please?"

"I don't know where to hide you," the frog said.

"Please hide me quickly," he said.

He said, "Just sit there. I'll do the talking. I'll gamble with her with my running. If she beats me, she can take you."

"How can this frog run?" the man thought to himself. He had his doubts.

Pretty soon the ghost-lady caught up to them. She was out

of breath and perspiring. She sure looked ugly now. "I'm looking for my husband," she said.

"He's sitting right here," Frog said. And she tried to grab him. The frog stopped her. He said, "We'll gamble for him. We'll race. If you beat me, you can have him."

Why did he say that? the man was thinking. *The frog can't run very fast.*

The frog said, "You just sit still." And he told the lady, "You stay here and stand still; I'm going to go make the trail where we will run, and when I get back, we'll race." So he went in one direction first, checking out the trail where they were going to run the race. Coming back, he made four places of quicksand, with his abilities as a frog, out of moisture. He made four pits of quicksand on the route where the woman was to run. This is what he did. Then he went back to the man and the woman.

"Okay," he said, "If you beat me, you take him. We'll go up to the other end and run toward this end, where the man is sitting." The woman agreed.

The man was sitting there waiting. "She won't beat me," the frog told him. The man was uneasy. Sweating it out because he didn't know about the pits the frog had made.

Then the two left and walked off to the far distance of the course, to run. The husband was to give the starting signal. He was to put his hand up and when he dropped it, they would run. He put his hand up and dropped it. The race was on. The frog was hopping away trying to get ahead. The woman took off and went straight toward the quicksand. In the first pit, she got into the quicksand up to her thighs. "What happened? What happened?" she started yelling. By this time, the frog had passed her. Hopped right past her, and kept on going. "What happened to me? What's going on?" she said. Then she finally got out and took off running again.

She was beginning to catch up with the frog. Just as she was about to catch up, she hit the second pit of quicksand. This time, she had a hard time; it was up to her waist. As she was trying to get out, the frog went ahead. Really took off. He was ahead and back in the race again. She tried and tried to get out, and finally did. She got out and took off running hard. She had almost caught up to the frog when she hit the third pit of quicksand. That's when she really had a hard time, struggling and fighting.

The frog was just about to catch up—"Go ahead and take off. She's still stuck," the man yelled to the frog. "You've got a good head start now. You can really take off and run now!"

"There's another grandfather living not far from here," the frog yelled back. "Go to him." The man took off running and headed for Jeddito. As he came up on that side, on the Keams Canyon side, he came to some Navajos.

The woman got caught in the last pit now, and she really got stuck deep this time. Finally, she got out, and the frog was waiting for her. The frog said, "I won." He said, "Go ahead and chase him now. I beat you and so I turned him loose."

And the man was way ahead now. Refreshed. But the ghost-woman started chasing him again. The man kept going. He ran and ran and ran into the flats. He saw two poles sticking out of the ground. When he got close, he found that it was a kiva. When he got to the kiva, he hollered in, "Ho!" There was just a "bratting" noise from inside. Twice he heard it. "Please hide me," he said. "There's a ghost-woman chasing me."

"What?" a voice said.

And he repeated it, "There's a ghost-woman chasing me."

And the voice said, "Come on in." And so he went in. "Come in, but come in the right way. Go around to the right-hand side of the kiva, and make your circuit. Clear around, and sit on this end, in the corner."

The man sits there, waiting. It was a ram that was in the kiva. Pretty soon he heard the ghost-woman hollering. "Ho!" The ram made the same "bratting" noise.

"Is my husband in there?" she asked.

"He's in here. Come on in," the ram told her.

"Okay," the woman said.

"Come in, and get him out," the ram said. And the woman started to go down the ladder. She took four steps on the ladder; then she got frightened for no reason, and she went back up. She tried to go in four times, but something frightened her each time. After the fourth time, she went in. Then she saw her husband sitting there. Boy, she sure looked terrible now, bushy-headed and all. The ram looked at the ghost-lady, then to the husband. He looked back and forth, and then said to her, "Don't bother him. You have to come into the kiva the correct way. You have to go around to the right and make your circuit."

As she was going around her circuit, the ram jumped on top of her and started having intercourse with her. The ram was doing this. And he kept it up and kept it up until she died. He screwed her to death. The ram was exhausted. They were just lying on the ground, inside the kiva. The man watched all this. He said "Well, he killed her."

Then the ram got up and the man said to him, "Thank you. I knew you would protect me, that's why I came in. I'm going now."

"You can't go yet," the ram said. "Sit down for a while and watch. I want to tell you something first," he said. "The woman was dead." The ram got up and went into the rear storage room of his kiva. He brought a small robe, a wedding robe, and covered the woman. "Just sit still and watch," he told the man. He went to the North. Stepped across the woman's body to the South. Then he went to the East and stepped across again to the West. Then he sat down and started singing, chanting. Kept chanting.

Pretty soon he went to the man. "You're coming here poorly," he said. "This is why everyone tells us a woman's word is not to be trusted. And you didn't believe it. Now you see what happens," he said. "Look at this robe now," he said. And then the robe started moving. Kept moving. Moving. Then he looked again; the woman bore four offspring.

The man said, "I'm afraid to lift up the robe."

"Don't be afraid. Go ahead and lift it. She won't do anything to you; I fixed her," he said. And the man went over. When he lifted the robe off the woman had turned into a goat. She had four young ones. This is how the goat was born on this planet.

So the ram told the man, "You take these, this mother goat and the children. Take them home. When you get home, you go ahead and take care of them. Tomorrow morning you kill one. Feed your family and your wife's family. These animals will never be gone. They will always exist."

The meaning was that they have gone to The Place of the Dead and returned. They're already dead, so they can't die again.

"They won't die out," he says. "This is how the goat was born." So the man took the goats out, and he started taking them back to the village. It was early morning when he left. By evening, he got back to the village. Below the Gap, there's a corral. It's still there. It's the oldest corral of the whole village. This is where he put the goats. Into the old corral. It's still there. The first corral. He put them in that corral.

When he got home, his in-laws were underfed. They were in very poor health. "My son-in-law, you got back!" the mother-in-law said.

"I've been away for quite a while," he said.

So he got home and he began thinking, "I went to a place where I shouldn't have been. But I saw the truth." This is what he was thinking. So he went to the back room to check where his wife's belongings were. There he found four caches of things that belonged to her. There were belts, buckskins, jewelry, mantas, beads, concho belts, and moccasins. And in the last hole, were personal belongings, rings and bracelets. She had been a rich woman, but now it all belonged to the husband. So he started taking them out. He took them all out and sold these things that had belonged to his rival, his wife's lover. And because of him, he was a rich man now. He sold the jewelry and other things and bought more sheep.

Early the next morning, he got up and went down to the corral. He picked out a young goat, took it home and cut its throat. He took everything out. They used everything, including the guts, "siihu." They boiled the meat and had a big stew. The old couple sure was hungry. They ate heartily. He brought them back to health—his wife's mother and father—because he brought the goats home. There was goat meat enough for all of them.

This is what we must remember: don't brush your hair at

night. Don't be mean. Don't go into witchcraft. And don't believe a woman's word. This is what he brought back from his journey to The Place of the Dead.

This is the end of my story.

Awatovi Story

Awatovi is a Hopi village, now a ruin, that was destroyed at the end of the seventeenth century, following the Pueblo Revolt of 1680. Numerous accounts give details of these events, including Harry C. James's Pages from Hopi History.

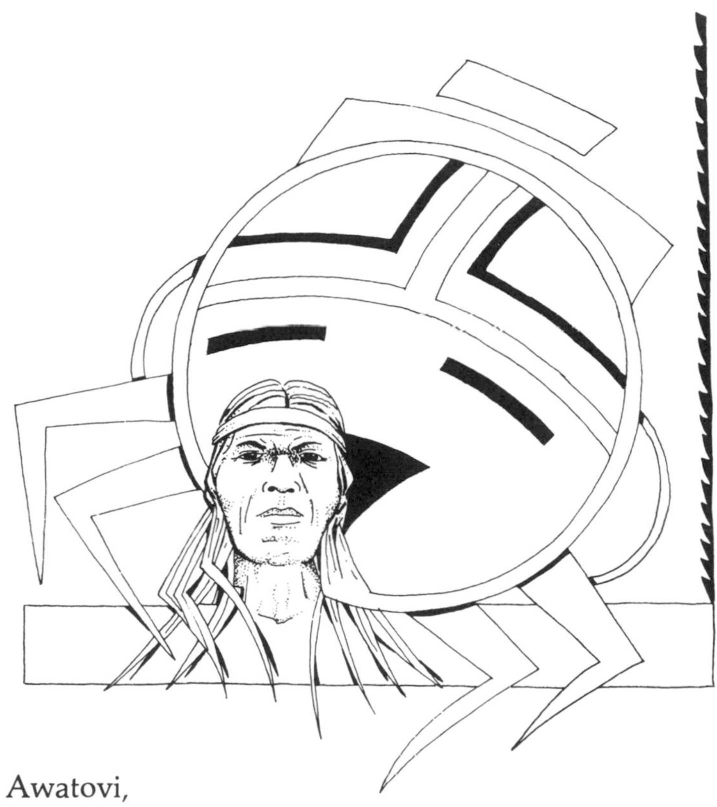

The chief of Walpi was angry.

This is my story. They lived a long time ago. In Awatovi, there was a large population of people. When they went to get wood, "Cheveyu Kachina" would kill them. People who went over there would never come back. He would always kill them. A person would be going to a place called New Spring to gather wood, and then the "Cheveyu" would kill him.

Then the people of Walpi heard about it. They heard that "Cheveyu" was killing people when they gathered wood. The son of the chief at Walpi didn't believe it, that "Cheveyu" was killing people. He wanted to find out for himself. He wanted to go gather wood. (He'd always carry wood in a cradle-like back pack.) So he went to his father and told him, "My father."

"What?" his father answered.

"I want to go get some wood and see if it's true that "Cheveyu" kills people over there. If it's true, I won't come back. Let me wear your good turquoise beads."

"You can't do that, my son. I'm stingy with you."

"Oh, I'll come back. It's not true. He won't do anything to me," the son said to the father. So he went after wood. He went early in the morning. He was supposed to get back by noon, so he left early in the morning.

He was gathering wood and making piles. He was about to tie them together and make a bundle so he could carry them, when something behind him made a noise. And he jumped. When he turned around, it was the "Cheveyu." "Cheveyu" was gathering wood himself. And carrying old wood on his back. And he always carries a knife. When the boy tried to get his wood, "Cheveyu" stabbed him. And the boy fell upon his wood.

"Cheveyu" took his turquoise beads. "This is what you want? You had no business not believing what you were told. This is what I will do to you." So he killed him.

And so the boy didn't return home. When he didn't get home by evening, the father got worried.

That was the first time that things didn't go right between the village of Walpi and Awatovi. Because the chief's son was killed. The chief of Walpi was angry.

Back at Awatovi, "Cheveyu" was walking away. Then he started to sing. He started to sing a song: "So ey yat tey, So ey yat te." And so on. You see, "Cheveyu" had killed the boy, so he was singing to the dead.

"So' yoko" is what the Navajos call him. "So' yoko" is what they call "Cheveyu." In the Navajo language, it means "I eat meat that is ground up." That's what Navajos call the "Cheveyu" in their own language.

When he didn't get home by evening, the father said, "I bet my son got caught at the New Spring area. Tomorrow I'm not going to eat and go look for him," he told his wife. "He never believes things that are told to him. He wore my turquoise beads, my really good turquoise beads."

So next morning, early in the morning, the father left. And he found the pile of wood and looked at it. All the wood was tied up, ready to be carried home. Then he found the young boy, his son. He felt around the neck. And there were no beads. He said, "'So' yoko' took the beads away." This is where he found "Cheveyu" singing his song to the dead boy.

"This is what happened. You wouldn't listen to me. Now I'm angry, and I'll do something to this village here, Awatovi," the father was crying to his son. "I'll have to just leave you here. This is what you wanted. So I'll bury you here. Something will happen to this village. Whoever that was that was dressed like that [impersonating the "Cheveyu"] was mean, and something will happen to him." So he made a shallow grave, and buried his son there and cried over the dead body.

And then the chiefs of the village of Walpi got together, and they talked. They talked about the "Cheveyu." They wanted to find out who it was. All of them were angry and wanted to do something to the Awatovi people. The Crier-chief was the one that calmed them down. "Don't do anything yet. This isn't the time yet. Something else is going to happen to the village yet." This is what the Crier-chief said to the boy's father, the chief of the village, "Kik mongqi."

That night they smoked together, and they talked to each other. So they got together with the chiefs of Awatovi. They talked to each other and tried to get things out of each other. "Yes. We don't know why this thing is walking around here; it's not us that are doing it. And we didn't ask anybody to do that. He's doing it to everybody. He's even doing it to people of our village. People go out to gather wood and don't come home. We were wishing that somebody would come and do him in. Take care of him, so that he won't be killing people any more. So this is how it will be. We will watch each other, take care of each other, and try to find out what it is that's around this area." So they said to each other, "We'll leave it as it is." They told the village chief of Walpi, "Take care of yourself and live strong. Something will come about. Whoever is doing this thing will reveal himself." So they left the village chief.

Later on, the people of Awatovi made their village chief's wife dance a public dance, and the chief was angered, the Awatovi chief. So he said, "My land is what I will give to anyone who will do away with my people here in Awatovi."

He went to different people with his proposal. The chief asked at different villages, but nobody would agree to do it. So he went to the Oraibi people, and the Oraibi people agreed to have a war with Awatovi. Then coming through Walpi, the Oraibi people stopped by the warrior society and asked them to join them. There were six who agreed to go. So they got together a war party and killed the people of Awatovi.

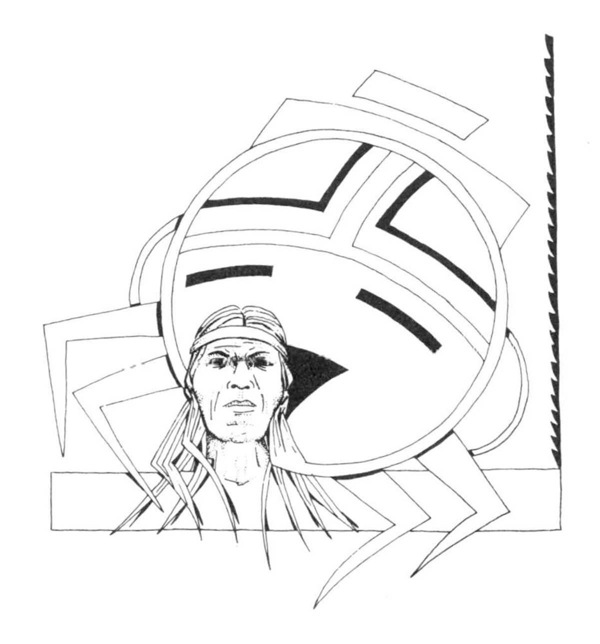

But when it was over, the Oraibi people weren't happy. "Why did we do this?" they said. "We can't go clear from Oraibi to this land to take care of it; it's too far away." They talked this over among themselves. So they gave the land to the warriors who participated from Walpi. The Reed Clan were the ones who were the warriors. So they accepted it. The Oraibi people were to use only the water at Awatovi. There was a lot of water there. Whenever they needed water for any use, they would have free access to it. This is the agreement they made.

So they said that Awatovi now belongs to the Walpis. "But

you people take care of it; it's good land. Plant on it. Don't build houses around the area because we won it; we didn't get it in the right way. So don't build houses around the area. Now that you have it, you have to put somebody out there to act as a lookout. A guardian of the place." This is what the Oraibis told the Walpis, the Reed Clan.

So the Reed Clan people are the ones who have authority of the land now. And they talked it over among themselves. They found an uncle among the Hano people, someone named Long Man. So he lived up there, and he had a peach orchard. He lived there until he died. He lived up by the spring, right above it. So for us, this man took care of the area and kept the Navajos away from it. And he lived up there until he died. This was my uncle, my grandmother's younger brother.

References

Driver, Harold E. *Indians of North America.* Chicago: The University of Chicago Press, 1961.

Gibson, Arrell Morgan. *The American Indian: Prehistory to the Present.* Lexington: D. C. Heath and Company, 1980.

James, Harry C. *Pages from Hopi History.* Tucson: The University of Arizona Press, 1979.

Simmons, Leo W., ed. *Sun Chief: The Autobiography of a Hopi Indian.* New Haven: Yale University Press, 1963.

Stewart, Tyrone, et al. *The Year of the Hopi.* Washington, D.C.: Smithsonian Institution Traveling Exhibition Service, 1981.

Yava, Albert, and Harold Courlander. *Big Falling Snow: A Tewa-Hopi Indian's Life and Times and the History and Traditions of His People.* New York: Crown Publishers, Inc., 1978.